Anna Maria Ortese

A Music Behind the Wall

Selected Stories

VOLUME ONE

Translated from the Italian

by Henry Martin

McPherson & Company

Translation copyright 1994 Henry Martin.
All rights reserved.
For information, address the publisher: McPherson & Company, Post Office Box 1126,
Kingston, New York 12401. Publication of this book has been assisted by grants from the
literature programs of the New York State Council on the Arts and the National Endow-
ment for the Arts, a federal agency. Designed by Bruce McPherson. Typeset in Bodoni
Book by Studio Graphics. The paper is acid-free to ensure permanence. Manufactured in
the United States of America.
1 3 5 7 9 10 8 6 4 2   1994 1995 1996 1997 1998 1999
fiRST EDITION

Library of Congress Cataloging-in-Publication Data

Ortese, Anna Maria.
    [Short Stories. English. Selections]
    A music behind the wall : selected stories / Anna Maria Ortese ;
    translated by Henry Martin.
    v. <1   > ; cm.
    ISBN 0-929701-39-9 (cloth) : $20.00
    1. Ortese, Anna Maria—Translations into English. I. Martin,
    Henry, 1942-   . II. Title.
    PQ4875.R8A25   1994
    853'.914—dc20   94-7229

"The Submerged Continent" was first published as "Il continente sommerso" in the collection *In sonno
e in veglia*, Adelphi, Milan, 1987. "Torture" was first published as "Supplizio" in the collection
L'infanta sepolta, Sera Editrice, Milan, 1950, and later in the collections *I giorni del cielo*, Mondadori,
Milan, 1958, and *L'alone grigio*, Valecchi Editore, Florence, 1969. "Fehla and the Melancholy Light"
was first published as "Solitario lume" in the collection *Angelici dolori*, Bompiani, Milan, 1937 and
1942, later in the collection *I giorni del cielo*, Mondadori, Milan, 1958, and finally, somewhat revised
and bearing the title "Fhela e il lume doloroso," as a section of the novel *Il Porto di Toledo*, Rizzoli,
Milan, 1975 and 1985. "Donat" was first published as "Le sei della sera," in the collection *L'infanta
sepolta*, Sera Editrice, Milan, 1950, subsequently as "6 della sera," in the collection *I giorni del cielo*,
Mondadori, Milan, 1958, finally as "Donat," in the collection *L'alone grigio*, Valecchi Editore,
Florence, 1969. "Winter Voyage" was first published as "Viaggio d'inverno" in the collection *L'alone
grigio*, Valecchi, Florence, 1968. "The Ombras" was first published as "Gli Ombra" in the collection
L'infanta sepolta, Sera Editrice, Milan, 1950, and later in the collection *L'alone grigio*, Valecchi
editore, Florence, 1969. "The Tenant" was first published as "Il signor Lin," in the collection
L'infanta sepolta, Sera Editrice, Milan, 1950, subsequently as "Il signor Lin," in the collection *I giorni
del cielo*, Mondadori, Milan, 1958, finally as "L'inquilino" in the collection *L'alone grigio*, Valecchi
Editore, Florence, 1969."Moonlight on the Wall" was first published as "La luna sul muro" in the
collection *La luna sul muro*, Valecchi, Florence, 1968. "The Tree" was first published as "L'albero"
in the collection *I giorni del cielo*, Mondadori, Milan, 1958, subsequently as "L'albero di neve," in the
collection *L'alone grigio*, Valecchi editore, Florence, 1969, and finally as "The Tree," (translated by
Henry Martin), in *New Italian Women*, ed. Martha King, Italica Press, New York, 1989. "The House
in the Woods" was first published as "La casa del bosco," in the collection *In sonno e in veglia*,
Adelphi, Milan, 1987.

CONTENTS

FOREWORD

Anna Maria Ortese's first volume of shorter fictions, *Angelici dolori,* appeared in 1937, her seventh and most recent, *In sonno e in veglia,* in 1987. The present collection of her stories in English translation ranges through the whole of these fifty years and touches nearly all the modes of storytelling which have characterized her creative life. The early work was once described as "magical realism." The middle period of work made that somewhat cumbersome adjective recede. The recent work lies at the edges of fable. Or perhaps it suggests the existence of a genre of "meta-fable" in which one listens to an otherworldly tale while casting a vigilant, questioning eye about the room in which it is being told. Rooms and houses are highly vital themes in Ortese's writing.

Anna Maria Ortese has remarked that her work is always and exclusively concerned with the inner life, and her stories most typically present us with moments in which the inner life might be said to readjust or realign itself, redefining its rights and prerogatives, reasserting its needs, re-establishing its proper scope—its sense of itself as a no less groundless than necessary function. This inner life with which the author deals is a complex world of thought, speculation and intuition, no less than of feeling and fantasy, and it touches dimensions that are more than simply personal. These stories, indeed, have little to do with psychology, since the psyche itself is the hero, focus or guiding principle of psychological narrative, whereas here the psyche is simply one force among many. Each of these stories is a place in which various realities manage to meet, or they concern themselves with voices and characters on whom such various realities converge. These realities themselves are the stories' truest protagonists. The psyche is simply the field, albeit an active field, in which their conjunctions and oppositions come momentarily into view.

Many of these stories have appeared on various occasions. In addition to presenting new stories, each of Ortese's collections of shorter fictions has furnished an occasion for the reappearance of previously published work. The author has a way of insisting on the continuity—even perhaps the simultaneity—of her present and her past. For example, one of the more recent stories in this present collection, "The Submerged Continent," seems to craft an emblematic bond between apparently different modes of relating to the self and the world: the deft and energetic thinking of the introduction and conclusion encircles and protects a much more ingenuous reverie which re-evokes the breathlessness of the author's earliest work. The narrative presents itself as a philosophical reflection on a dream, but it also engages the theme of "the ages of man," and its strategy for doing so lies partly in deploying its own internal moods and styles as elements of a startling yet self-evident continuum. This story is in some ways reminiscent of the author's most curious and *sui generis* novel, *Il porto di Toledo*, which was published in the early 1970s. *Il porto di Toledo* re-appropriated the stories of *Angelici dolori* and used them as elements of a fictional investigation into the life of the girl who had written them some forty years previously. The author's vision of the inner life is both dynamic and conservative. Nothing can be taken for granted, and nothing can be overlooked.

Ortese once wrote that her work can be seen as falling into two basic categories: the callow and the unfashionable. Those words sound barbed and inauspicious, but so purposely so as finally to remind us of a more serene statement by Tommaso Landolfi: that literature starts where literature stops. This, perhaps, is the greatest of the great romantic longings which have survived into the modern age. Anna Maria Ortese's goal, as voiced in one of her stories, is to reach and explore those "regions of the soul where everything impossible in fact takes place," and no secondary description of what and how she writes, even if quipped by the author herself, can be anything more than secondary. Yet wherever she goes is a place from which she always returns: each of these stories is a round-trip ticket from a here to a there (an extraordinary there) and back again to here—but always with a difference, a loss of ignorance and innocence; or through their loss the rediscovery of the greater innocence of a greater openness to experience.

Henry Martin

The Submerged Continent

- like Mattia Pascal

I am convinced that most of the <u>evils</u> afflicting the world derive from its inhabitants' <u>lack of a commonly shared culture</u>. The world until now has been divided into races, even if ideas of class have recently been assumed more central. Class, however, is nothing more than a *racial* division within a people, and since race is wholly a question of culture, class too corresponds to levels and degrees of culture. A child—no matter where that child is born—can grow up to be *Chinese* or *Turkish* or *Brazilian* or *Swedish*, quite indifferently; and independently of his or her social origins, that child, on reaching adulthood, can just as easily become a professor of fine arts, or a senator, or an illustrious surgeon, or a florist—or, on the other hand, a chronic inmate of the prisons. Everything depends upon the persons who surround the child from the time of his or her first babblings, and on the notions that he or she is taught, along with the kind of nourishment and the more or less good habits that accompany his or her growth. This principle deserves the closest attention of everyone concerned with government, from economists to politicians: the principle that <u>culture alone is the force that shapes or eliminates races and classes</u>, and that the goal of a happier, more tranquil world (which all of us want) can only be achieved by taking up the task of disseminating the basic principles of culture.

But please don't misunderstand me. When I use the word "culture," I am not at all referring to the endless stock of notions that derives from the various fields of knowledge, and from all its categories and specializations. To imagine the speedy diffusion of any such form of culture—in the space, say, of twenty years (a blink of the eye for the younger generations)—would surely be naive. And even if it might be accomplished, the result would be downright harmful. No. Every human being, in order to be truly a human being, has to search out *the greater part* of his or her culture entirely on his or her own. And less of it, in the end, is better than more. Which is not a self-contradiction. The important part of culture—the part of culture that ought to be imparted to all human beings, just like their mothers' milk—consists after all of the basic principles of knowledge, of which there are not very many (on the order of nine or ten), and they can fit, as here you see, onto any page of notebook paper.

First: *where* we are, and who we are. On this score, every child should be informed right from the start that the Earth is a ball *suspended* in space, a modest pebble lost within a universe which in turn is lost among other universes; then they need to be advised that it is *very unlikely*, no matter how potent the tools possessed by the last man on earth, that we will ever know the nature of these other universes; the next thing they ought to be exposed to is the notion that something *infinite* and *secret* (even perhaps benevolent, though any such surmise is far from certain) hovers above us. Tell them as well that all human beings— father, grandfather, and the new-born child, mother, and the unknown stranger—belong to the great family of Life, which is the only family we know; and that it also includes

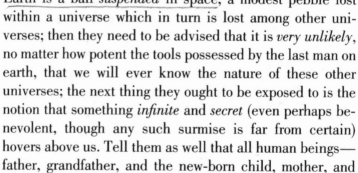

all the animals, even the insects. And that every blow we strike against life must therefore rebound against us; that we have to respect and nurture life if we ourselves desire to be respected and nurtured.

We can leave aside the list of the seven or eight other principles. They ought to derive in any case from the first ones already mentioned, likewise engendering respect for the Earth as our only raft in the sea of eternal nights that lie around us—and love, and compassion for life, no matter the condition (even exalted) in which it finds itself.

Since a certain belligerence is typical of human beings, a belligerence mainly vented by wars and amorous intrigues, still more so by competition; and since both belligerence and competition are a drive—unconsciously— to aggress and prevail: well, children should first be given a hint of the instruments with which to express—and therefore to free—the unconscious: the principles of painting, as one sure example, and of music: the colors and the drum. Then furnish every means for the satisfaction of the inborn impulse to run, to make oneself agile and beautiful: the hoop, the ball, the boat, and especially the kite and swimming. At the same time teach defense against illness: hygiene, the balanced use of one's own body; its finely calibrated mechanisms should of course be explained, the functioning of its various parts, its liability to wear and tear. Breathing and the circulation of the blood should be presented as holding first place, since they are the seat— if practiced well—of all the virtues: from clemency (anger is bad for the health), to temperance (moderation in the use of the body maintains and increases its life expectancy). Concerning sex, the only thing to say is what it is: a mechanism present in all the forms of life for the reproduction of its various species, and the use of which is connected to precisely this necessity of preserving life by way of self-reproduction. If, on the other hand, one has no desire to reproduce oneself, one can do without it, consecrating the mind (sex is activated by the mind) to other equally auspicious activities. But the best thing of all would be to teach that the sexual life obscures and precludes, as a rule, the cognition of love. Such cognition has its seat in the dreams, and these dreams are no empty divagations of the mind, but constitute a sort of bridge by way of which the individual, stepping outside of the definitions of specific organic determinacy, can reconnect with the sources of life: sources that perhaps are lost in the cosmos, but from which we come and to which we hope (no matter how impossible it seems) to return. Dreams are of two types: some are reproductions of mental events and objects, whereas others are alien to such objects and events; these latter have the name of *inspiration*, and they hold the command and the guide to cosmic life. The alien dreams are the allies of the human being: the bringers of the arts and of prophecies, the ambassadors of destiny, guides to a day and a place which are truly real (as these are not, since they are transient). Guides to the immortal. And even if what I call "the immortal" is still no indisputable certainty, that fact is of no importance. My belief, however, is that is does exist. Otherwise, why would we have a name for it?

What is love? Love is that highest peak of experience where the more than natural—the Stranger—establishes contact with the merely human, through the agency of an indescribable emotion. Like a thunderbolt, this emotion discharges through the whole of the body (heart, breathing, mind), increasing the tempo of its life. Sexuality, too, bends to this command. Love, in fact, on its very rare visits to the earth, also passed—since it invades the whole human being—through our mechanisms of reproduction, stamping them forever with the mark of joy. In the absence of true and proper love (which is a genie and appears no more than once in any millennium) sexuality preserved its memory, and thus grew precious to the human race. But constant confusion has since arisen with respect to the god and the altar, the spirit and the letter; and that temple—since the genie has been missing for centuries—has turned into a place of buying and selling. Whereas it ought to be pledged to modest and simple rites, and to freedom from falsehood. Love, moreover, one fine day—if the human race survives—will choose a different seat in the human body: the eyes, perhaps, or the mind. Human life may one day express its greatest tenderness through the eyes and the mind. And life may effect its reproduction through thoughts and glances charged with emotion and unfathomable delicacy.

So, I don't mean to say at all that love should be prohibited; but its name must not be spoken in vain, and children are not to be hoodwinked with mendacious idols. And the difference between false and authentic love, Oh Stranger, is seen in this one fact: that false love is happy, and true love (a gift borne by the Stranger) is sad. The first, in fact, exists for the purpose of continued terrestrial generation; the latter establishes contacts (fortuitous, in this terrestrial life) with the place from which we came. Another significant particular: love between persons of the same age, or who in general are peers and equals, is terrestrial. Since the genie of love is a bringer of commands and a force that alters the terrestrial, he is partly destructive from terrestrial points of view. He enters terrestrial experience as mourning and death. Divine visitation bodes no good for common men; therefore it cannot be protracted. Veritable love promptly transfigures and kills old men. And love reveals its authenticity in yet another fact: it founds ideas rather than families.

* * *

Returning to ignorance—and to its widespread presence even among persons whom we think of as cultured, or at least who know how to read and write—I'd like to mention a very curious fact: there are people who still know nothing about certain electrical or magnetic phenomena, for example what lightning is. And at as late an age as eighteen, when they appear already to know everything, it then turns out that they believe a bolt of lightning to be a rod of *iron* hurled down against the earth (with uncanny violence) by a hurricane. This, indeed, is what I myself, who now am writing these lines, believed: and I was precisely eighteen years old.

Again on human ignorance (and on the state in which the author has found, and continues still today to find herself): the Past! Most human beings, if you question them, know that the past is what was, while yet believing that at present it is still to be found "somewhere." Nothing might be more ridiculous; and yet I have every right to speak of it since I myself have held such thoughts. Up until two years ago I was convinced that all of the Past was *gathered together* in some part of life or the cosmos. Though I couldn't be clear as to whether that place was spiritual or physical, I imagined it still to hold *everything* that had ever happened and of which we know through chronicles and mementos: Greece, Rome, the Middle Ages; Christopher Columbus, Pizarro, Cortez, the ancient Peru of the Incas; and so on and so forth, all the way to the great writers and poets (and their civilizations); to the eighteenth-century France of Voltaire and Rousseau; to the America of the Pilgrim Fathers and its first cities, to the story of General Lee; to all of nineteenth-century America, and on to the nineteen thirties. I didn't forget Napoleon's gesture of taking the crown from the hands of the pope, in the midst of a splendor and a feast of faces and days that we find it nearly impossible to imagine. And there was no excepting England's eighteenth century, with its luminous vitality; or its nineteenth-century storms and the way they were treated in the writings of authors whose works we hold dear. Those same men and women who bear the names of Defoe, Dickens, Coleridge, the enchanting Jane Austen, or the Brontë family (names chosen at random). So I could really remain quite calm while surveying a present that grew ever more vile, confused, and unfree, remarking to myself (in my dream-filled mind): yes, but still, in spite of everything, *they*—along with their peoples and their temples of light— *are there.* "There, *where*, my dear?" someone might have asked me, but I lived in such thorough darkness that this sad question was never addressed to me. And then one day (quite by chance—or was it some genie that guided my hand?) I picked up and opened an ancient book: Lucretius. And the truth advanced to meet me in all its devastating power: you're to understand, dear soul, that there exists nowhere at all a place in which one finds that past so dear to you; nor will it ever revive, never, ever again.

It was summer, as I quite well remember, and the days were mellow: hot, a gentle wind, a blank light that covered the world with a patina of sleep. And there I sat, next to a fireplace now devoid of fire, with this excruciating certainty: that the Past *no longer exists and will never return*!

Along with this crushing blow, still others were then to present themselves, guided again by Lucretius: that the Future, the brother of the past, is likewise non-existent, as physical reality; it is barely an hypothesis, just as the past is memory. Only the Present would remain. But my spirit, so suddenly dazzled by truth, quite clearly saw that even the present has no substance, and is only an imaginary line

17

between those other two states; or, to put it better: the last swell of memory as illuminated partly by the already extinguished past, partly by the non-existent and only putative future. Therefore no past, therefore no future, therefore no present; nothing at all (Lucretius made clear) but *unending matter*, the persistence of which gives *time*. So trees, animals and human beings are nothing but TEMPORARY phenomena of matter. I braved the thought that non-existence was now the lot not only of so-called "historical" reality (which in fact is memory) but as well of "common" reality: there is only matter, and within this matter lies the memory of what it was or of what one presumes it will be. And the self, I asked myself at a certain point, does at least the self exist? But I awaited a reply which never came: through the open windows, nature exploded in a luxury of leaves and songs of wandering birds; there were also butterflies (but not brightly colored) passing uncertainly by, as though drunk, in the light wind. I alone, it seemed to me, was acquainted with this mourning of the spirit.

Such a sad day! And such other sad days that followed! Pain accompanied me everywhere: the Past does not exist! We'll not worry too much about the Future! But the Past, with its mysterious epochs, sparkling in the darkness of dreams; the Past with its pageants and seas; the Past with its splendid pirate ships, their sails unfurled on a dark blue sea, the Past with all its continents and everything that constituted history—the Past with its palaces, its gardens, its halls, its gowns, its feathers, songs, wars, and stories both famous and unknown: the Past no longer exists. Those women, those men no longer exist. And as if that weren't enough, not even the present is real, since continually, behind the backs of everyone, it precipitates into death, into darkness: it's like the wake of a ship, an always fainter wake.

Now, precisely this image of a ship and its wake came to my aid. I was rescued by the thought that human history—which I bewailed because I loved it and wished it never to end—might belong to Lucretius' matter as something extraneous to matter itself, as a kind of light, a *sign* that is never—truly—to be found in a given place, but that moves on a dark and infinite sea (of matter) *without*, however, being swallowed by matter; and that extraneous something—even though it leaves no furrow—remains entirely self-contained, and was, and therefore is: that extraneous something (extraneous to the pure materiality of atoms) is the consciousness—a separate reality—of matter itself, and consisted of what we refer to as spirit. It was spirit (I thought).

But the question remained as to whether such spirit sprang up from matter or traversed it. Was it matter's most essential content, or something *alien* to matter? And this was a question to which I couldn't respond; it was quite beyond me, since I am a person like so many others, with a limited mind that's unaccustomed to higher mathematics—even, indeed, to lower mathematics—and capable only of frail, halting perceptions. And what difference did it make? I had managed already to reach one conclusion (farewell, sweet past, my pride, my light): that history *is* spirit at work in matter, that such matter therefore reveals a spirit, that this spirit is the self of the human being and the animal and the plants and all living creatures, and that through man this spirit examines, reviews, and *criticizes* history. And all the same without repudiating history. How could one repudiate one's own memory? Spirit, moreover, can be seen to be alive by virtue of its distance from all futile preoccupation with collecting the *matter* of the past, since that matter by now is already a void; equally from making calculations on the future, since future matter is still a void;

likewise from taking pride in the present, which is only memory and hypothesis; it's alive (this spirit) in so far as it scrutinizes the matter of the world, examines the thing called matter and its limits, and measures itself eternally against these things: the *memory* of matter (or history); and the true essence of matter, which is to say, precisely, matter as the stream-bed of philosophy. The spirit, I said to myself, captains the ship called time, and it has to devise the instruments that permit such navigation (through eternity); and such instruments, yes, lie in science and its various minor reaches—let's say a bit of technology, a bit of economics—but their guide remains philosophy.

On the following days I returned to this concept, the concept of philosophy—or of the study of the things which pre-exist the human being, attempting to discover their laws, and therefore the laws as well of human life—and I realized that not only does philosophy not exclude reason, but indeed is reason's guide, since reason is only the emergent part, so to speak, of the human intellect—of that ship which is the human spirit—and philosophy is the part that lies beneath the surface, in contact with all of life's coldest or more fiery parts. And philosophy is also an antenna, or a kind of radar: reason sails by night, gazing at the stars; and when reason gets lost in a night of fog, philosophy will tell it where monsters and reefs and imminent hurricanes lie. Philosophy is prudent, as well as benevolent: it *will not run aground* on those reefs, and it *will not kill those monsters.* It will simply avoid them.

But where the ship of the human spirit—guided by memory, philosophy and benevolence—is going, is something I don't know, nor could anyone say with certainty. Surely, however, it is going somewhere. So now, on this particular subject, let's listen to the sad and yet gentle voice of dreams.

I don't want to talk about all the dreams we dream when we're asleep. As said before, they are largely objective, a memory of the facts and events of the day. I want only to talk about dreams which come from outside, from the parts of ourselves we have lost, meaning our past, the time that no longer exists: dreams which sometimes seem to bring us news of an unknown land where that past would appear to have gone, thus encouraging philosophy's hopes for a true and effective reality which reason, as evidenced, most energetically denies. But whether that reality finds its source in what lies before or at back of the spirit—whether it itself is matter or spirit—we do not know. We only know that it is sweet and sad.

There are people who once again visit with the dead, seeing loved ones "as though alive, and smiling so serenely," they say. There are others who see things that later truly happen: like tomorrow's events or people they will meet. Often such dreams (as though ashamed, or for some profounder reason) are masked *as something else*. You see a bird build its nest in your room, and a flock of birds in agitation, and a swallow flying back and forth from the fireplace to the table. Strange, isn't it? Yet you know it's no question of a swallow, and that someone in fact is trying to send you a message! And perhaps that someone is no longer among the living. You know it without at all knowing it: that is the mystery.

Where do such dreams come from? A mystery, if all we knew were what in fact we know: the knowledge that the past and future do *not* exist. And if they do exist, then certainly not as anything material, or as any actual thing that lies ensconced in any given place. Yet who can say that as a kind of *scripture* engraved in matter, or as some other different reality that traverses matter, they do not still (or already) exist?

As you see, I can reason quite clearly; but then, suddenly, I abandon reasoning and spin off speculations from such frail, cherished, delirious, and sinister facts. (Sinister, since where we are is to the right of them!)

I want to recount a dream. I don't know why, but it's a dream I continually dream. I think myself capable of dreaming others, yet this is the only one that comes to me.

There was a family in Naples, when I was a teenage girl, an illustrious, princely family with which, quite by chance, I had come to be friendly. Though wealthy, the members of this family lived modestly in an unobtrusive mansion among the narrow lanes. The father, the prince, was a very distinguished man, and highly refined. The mother, simple and plain, had a great talent for everything, and a soul which was very dear to me. The three daughters of the household, whose names for the moment I will not mention, were also dear to me. And, in my eyes, beautiful: they had that very special grace which can often illumine the lives of girls who as women will be nothing special. They were also good, or appeared so to me. In truth, I can only describe them as phenomena of the spirit (in matter), since even in spite of seeing them frequently, I never learned, nor attempted to learn, anything personal about them.

The oldest girl was very wise and strong, and showed a generous smile. The second was a little beauty, transparent and delicate. I felt she knew everything, including everything about me. The third girl escapes me; but I seem to remember an air of great strength and vivacity She had brown plaits. All three of them were between fifteen and nineteen years old, no older. They were the life and the pride of the whole house.

Now, during the war, and somewhat earlier, this family was under surveillance, owing to their ideas, which was something that I myself, having no ideas at all (this was the time when I thought of bolts of lightning as iron rods falling from the skies), did not know. I went to their home the way one visits a public park. I'd enter a room and take a seat on a bench, I'd think or look out the window. Sometimes I would write. Sometimes I met their Highnesses, the father and mother, and immediately rose to my feet. But when the daughters came in, I'd often remain seated.

What did we talk about? Who knows! About our feelings, about the things we were going through at that particular time. But never about facts; facts were private. But multitudes of fancies on our feelings and dreams. Sometimes, I would also sleep over in that house. A bed would be prepared for me in one of the studies, and the three girls, towards eleven o'clock—perhaps it was raining outside, or the garden was surmounted by a wonderful moon—would come to say good-night to me. One of them would sit on the bed, another would kneel on the carpet, the other would hold my hands. Carla, the oldest girl, said to me one evening:

"Tell me, dear, quite frankly, what you think of us? *Who*, in reality, would you say we are?"

I had never thought about that. I jokingly replied:

"You're my friends."

"But in reality, in addition to being your friends—which is an attribute," said the sweet and cultivated Carla, "who are we? *Inside* of us."

"Truth? Goodness?" said the pretty one (whose name was Alina) as a jest.

The youngest (named Nera) stressed the syllables with great precision: "Haven't you dreamt us?... Aren't you simply, perhaps, dreaming about us, whereas we in fact... *non-existent?*"

23

This tender phrase moved me more than all the others.

"No...real...as much as I am, my dears," or some similar expression, I replied with a smile. And then, as their darting shadows projected very large—owing to a hidden light—on the white walls, and skidded back and forth: "But one doesn't see life very clearly, when one is young...." I happily remarked.

"That's true...quite true!" said the youngest girl, looking at me gravely.

Carla came to touch my forehead, fleetingly.

"Never betray us, please!" she said gently.

And how might I have done such a thing?

"We'll see each other again some day...believe me," she then remarked, very moved.

As she left the room, she once again turned her lovely face in my direction, while her younger sisters, more girlish, embraced me before departing. And:

"Haven't you dreamt us?"

outside realm of fact

"Truth? Goodness?"

"Never betray us, please!" they sadly entreated.

When the three sisters had gone, I immediately felt drowsy and fell asleep; but shortly afterward I awoke again and looked around me: the moon flooded across the garden and in through the open window: the bed, the walls, the room's two very severe doors were brightly lit. The silence was absolute, but for a rustle here and there of leaves in the garden, stirred by the wind which is always present in these fierce nocturnal solitudes—and the three girls seemed, indeed, to my inanimate memory, non-existent. Then, replacing them, came another image, which at the time was very precious to me. I won't say whether it was of a man or a woman; that isn't necessary. It bore a friendly smile and repeated the three girls' words: as though the three girls had been the dream, and this fourth figure were now the reality

24

of what they symbolized. Again the same grave words:

"Haven't you dreamt us?"

"Truth? Goodness?"

"Never betray us, please!"

And certainly the figure didn't take me by the hand, but indeed retreated; and there were harbors and lights at its back. Then flotillas of armies. Then hell. Then the moon and peace returned, but without my being aware of it. I didn't awake until the following morning, and I didn't remember a single word, nor the scene itself, for a very long time.

Now, during the war I lost a great many people, relatives or simply friends; and above all else I lost a large part of myself. Even language was no longer the same. I imagine that everyone shared this experience, and even if they felt themselves to be the very same people as before, that sensation was a dream. Absentminded and listless, I walked about barefoot across the earth; I encountered people, yet for me these people were lost. Thus, one day, I saw the three girls again, in their mansion where nothing had changed (it seemed) in a life lived out with the jovial princes—their mother and father—and the faithful servants. I was hurt that they didn't enquire as to where I had been, or ask how much of myself I had lost. But only to a certain degree. Time had passed over them (weakening recall of that evening and the sacred questions of the dream) just as it had passed over me: I too no longer remembered those questions, or my fragile but tender words of reply.

We parted as strangers and never met again.

Now—and this is where I find the mystery—why ever, now toward the end of my life, should these three girls return so frequently in dream, always kind and enigmatic:

"Haven't you dreamt us?"

"Truth? Goodness?"

"Never betray us, please!"

And while speaking and hearing these words, we always—I have had this dream year after year, ever since the onset of Italy's new way of life—we always walk in some rainy night through the sublime, melancholy city of our youth. We never say anything else. But whenever I see these girls in my dreams, I immediately feel that it isn't a dream: I could never call it an illusion. I feel that something within me truly catches a glimpse of a distant time—a time deprived of matter—and such time is the pure yearning of the heart towards its origins…its unspeakably glorious, unknown origins. And there are moments when I feel that for *them* it makes no difference: they come from the abyss (the wake of the ship), and they ask:

"What did you think of us, my dear?"

"There has been no betrayal," I sometimes reply, and I can feel with what attention they listen to me.

"It was not I, my dears, who betrayed you—if betrayal is a word for speaking of an absence—but life that moves and passes, bringing vast changes everywhere around us."

"Yes, that's true, that's true!" remarked Carla during one of our recent encounters, there in that region beyond the day. And tonight, suddenly, she said to me:

"You haven't asked about Daddy."

"I already know," I replied, "and concerning your precious mother as well."

"That they are no longer here beneath the sun."

"Yes," I replied.

"But somewhere, no?" said Nera.

And Alina: "Would you know where?"

The eyes of their youth (immortal, somewhere or another) held a sparkle.

"Don't cry," I said, "my dears."

* * *

And once, just last week, I met the prince and princess in person.

They were strolling along a street not far from their home, which, strangely, no longer stood beside a lane, but facing the sea: a celestial marina. All the balconies of the yellow houses, here and there, were in flower. With pink and red geraniums! One overheard the music of an organ grinder. I won't repeat the words of the song, but they were full of a heavy happiness, of longing for the past, of laughter as well as tears.

"Good day!" I said.

"Now just how long has it been since we have seen each other?" asked the princess.

"You're still studying, no?" enquired the prince with his wry good humor. I found him to have aged a great deal.

"Yes, I certainly am."

"Fine, how very fine...." As always, he wasn't really interested, but he liked to be kind to the friends of the family.

All the same he seemed a bit lost.

"How much time has slipped away," he suddenly avowed, with a touch of sadness, "since the last time we saw you."

"Thirty...or something like it," said the mother.

"Come to dinner tonight...if you can...and your family, are they well?"

I reply—with compassion—that they are.

"Well, remember, my dear, to give them our best."

They resumed their walk, but seemed to hesitate.

The princess then turned back around:

"If you see our daughters...please: say hello to them for us...."

She wiped away a tear.

* * *

Now, what's to be said about this—that's the question which comes to mind—this appearance and re-disappearance of derelict souls, which is now what the prince and princess are? And why should they ask me to take their greetings to other derelict souls? Why can't they simply talk on their own with their girls—who, moreover, by now are no longer girls? Why should they appeal to me? But, of course: our homes and houses have been destroyed, the years have passed, the city has altered, all of us, who were yesterday's girls and boys, are growing old, and yet they still return... as though time hadn't passed, or were stored away in some place to be reached by way of dreams. But those times remain UNCHANGED!

In this case, I say to myself, if something of life nonetheless remains, and even perhaps all of it, won't that life—precisely because it remains unchanged—be a new container of the good and evil that was, and therefore heaven and hell? Won't life's powerful continue to live in their evil, and innocents in their pain? And can it be right for this to happen, if it happens? That the past—if it still exists, which I do not believe—should be immutable?

On this score, Reader, there remains a small and not inconsequential observation, if you chance to thirst for hope and virtue, for the transformation of evil into good, and cannot content yourself with the tenebrous continents of history. You will have noticed a sadness in the prince and princess, on the occasion when I met them in my dream, the sadness of their utterly worldly, utterly conventional parting words: that greeting: "If you see our daughters...please: say hello to them for us...."

So they won't be seeing their daughters this evening! That invitation to dinner was pure, sad fantasy.

* * *

Yes, I say to myself again, most probably they *couldn't* behave in any other way—so *conventionally*. But they *know* that time passes. And if they *know*, then they truly exist. Yes, they do exist! And if they exist, it then perhaps is possible that spirit, of which we were speaking before, is more than memory alone; it would also be *an act:* an eternal act of choice, of love. And all, truly all of its component creatures would be hidden away in some place within that spirit—a spirit which in fact is a submerged continent—no longer a fragile ship…. And there they wait: for something that finally, at the end of everything, will bring them all back together. writing art bring them back together

I have finished. It is daytime. I don't want to think any more, not for now. But I want to add before closing that this does not strike me—none of the things up until now supposed—as unreasonable. And perhaps…perhaps the spirit is not a ship, but simply *a voyaging continent, a submerged continent!* Hidden! It seems to be a ship, but only because it moves, and little of it emerges. But it's a continent, hidden and grandiose!

One day we will see its shores, its palms.

Yes, we will see each other again—my dear, grave, and tender girls of the past, the noble prince and princess, the delicate night-time shadows of the Neapolitan mansion. All of us, and others as well. We'll embrace one another again, my dears.

I send you—from the day, from the sea, from this terrible, monotonous sound of waves, from nothingness—my tender, festive, immortal and devoted salute.

Torture

A human being can encounter so many states of wretchedness and terror, so many different horrors: to stand alone at the center of a mob that awaits excitedly to see you subjected to an instrument of torture; or to kneel in the shadow of a scaffold where a brother or a friend stands pale and dazed at its summit; or to find yourself closed up in a room some Sunday evening, listening back to the music of youth. We can also go suddenly blind, or lose arms and legs in accidents; the tongue that offers harmonious sound to the feelings and thoughts that gently surge within the brain, can be ripped out by bandits. And that is not all. Human beings can find themselves constrained to look on powerless, and with no recourse other than to tremble with fear, as their home collapses, or as their city is razed by enemy fire. And later they can gape at pestilence—abetted by the riot and poverty entrained in the invaders' aftermath—as it then takes possession of the city's populace like flames amidst dry grass, devouring their bodies with its ponderous tongue. They can witness how a place which once was the home of peace, a place which rang with the blameless gaiety of song and country dances, turns now into a realm only of tears, mourning, and desolation. The Moon on some May evening that troubles the dreams of the world of men and beasts may

31

even collapse from her niche in the heavens, may plummet with a host of stars that deck the sky, and screaming and flaming extinguish herself as she falls among the trees. The very air will die from it; and what once was the smooth calm sea will swell and rush with thunder towards the shore, crashing against it and roiling beyond it, changed into a myriad of bright green horses, their nostrils foaming with columns of water while they gallop upon the villages to drown out houses, churches and theaters, submerging the squares, encircling the forests and sucking them below, engulfing the flanks of the mountains. The mountains will split, quaver and crumble; the birds and changing clouds that lived at their peaks will rush away in the blackness of precocious night to carry news of the scourge to the lands as yet unapprised of it. And again that is not all. A man can be stricken by divine malediction and witness the corruption of his still living flesh; caress his body's leprous wounds; or tremble as he feels within his bones the rising fire, reckless and unrestrained, of a fever from which no one can save him. Or a sword may be plunged into his belly and slowly search upwards for his liver or his heart as he vainly invokes the name of God. Or again…. Such are but a few of the countless plagues that can blast a human life. Yet nothing, on reflection, in the list of all these horrors can rank as more tremendous, as a more gruesome and silent, a more savage and penetrating torture than the affliction of the lover whose love is not returned. I can conceive of no more evil plight, of no more abysmal route to the inward experience of catastrophe. For the lover who knows such grief, pain, and bewilderment is subject to a singular rupture of the balance of nature, to a convulsive unreasonability that can tyranize a human life: though the faculties of feeling and perception remain intact, the organs of the lover's body, the very blood, every fiber of the flesh and especially the heart are displaced into those of the person adored. Each and every part of such a lover is entrusted to the whim and good graces of another—often an unknown stranger—who takes little account of the moment of the life in his custody. Mostly that stranger will find it an annoyance of which quite happily and hastily to be rid, and no matter if his hands in the meantime run with blood, or if the lover's face and members, stripped rudely off and cast aside, have been crushed into ribbons of tattered flesh. Yet the mind of the victim will find no cause for hate or thoughts of vengeance. It would be easier for a child to devour its mother, or for the earth to confound the sky, or for clouds to lend support to animals and trees than for the lover to address reproof to the beloved. Hours and even whole days will pass in which the creature whose soul lies wholly in the hands and caprice of another remains entirely lifeless, or with only so tiny a remnant of life as allows that soul, with never a word or a sigh, to witness its own ruination. If the beloved were only for a instant to remember, to perceive the lover, supine and dying on a narrow bed, incapable of words or thought, and to bestow a sign of pity—that would be enough. The lover would breathe a sigh of profound liberation. Yet that person is highly unlikely to remember, and will never take notice until the victim's capacity for suffering approaches exhaustion and collapses towards livid death. Then, perhaps, the beloved will smile; and the lover whose head has already dropped, no longer able to part swollen lips, will raise that head and offer difficult gratitude. No longer to own a single part of one's own body, not an arm, a hand, a finger, nor even a scrap of tongue, nor the pupil of an eye; to own no organ with which to see, to call out, to scream or to defend oneself; to find oneself entirely in the power of the indifference or cruelty of a creature who does not know us, a creature for whom we do not exist: how desperately painful, and yet how frequent and familiar.

The man or the woman we love isn't simply a person with whom we'd desire an hour of delight; such a person is a great deal more than that; such a person is what a mother is to a newborn child. We need the heat, the gentle words, the lilt, the deep, peaceful, endlessly tender gaze. Yet the gift doesn't come when we need it, but at whim, when it's no bother.

To rip away the mother from a child a few months old, a child whose life depends on her, would seem to be a strange and unusual crime. Yet similar events take place quite normally. The man or the woman we love is again our mother, but with a difference; not being in any way tied to us, she can watch with indifference as we perish. Persons who suffer from such an atrocious disease have been known at times to wail and scream, appealing with all the strength of their voices to the man or the woman who holds their existence in the palm of a hand. But most neither scream nor even continue to think; their being, if some part of it is not yet cold and inert, does nothing but reverently murmur the name they adore. The *mother*, the person who gives them life, almost never so much as approaches them, mysteriously, inwardly, enjoying the terror which makes them mute; taking delight in the torture to which his or her indifference subjects a living creature. Independent of a person's morals, which may even be perfect, and independent of a person's will, which may even be pure, the interior of the human being contains a hunger for suffering; and to avoid doing damage to the person who feels it, this hunger sates itself on others. To take possession of an individual by pretending affection, and then to repudiate that person, proving his dependence and then stripping him away from us, is one of the most refined of systems.

Compassion is such a wonderful quality in a living

creature. That compassion which is not born from weakness or fear of punishment, or from some dark and remote suspicion of the existence of a law of retribution, but simply from the evaluation and condemnation of acts that bring unhappiness to another creature—especially if that creature is defenseless and lies within our power! To find someone who takes no intimate pleasure, unobserved by all, from seeing another being fallen and in pain; who feels an inward shiver of revolt at such a spectacle, and who desires to remedy it—I believe there is nothing else on earth that would merit being called divine.

But intelligence on the one hand, and weariness on the other, usually transform the human heart into a kind of tumor, a sweet and poisonous excrescence, and the brain into a labyrinth of perversity. In what part of a being so ruined by experience and disappointment, in a being that finds its key in itself and its own exclusive interests, can there be a place for compassion? So alas for anyone whose life depends upon another, who has unreflectively chosen a mother—for those who in other words have delivered themselves to a guide whose immaculate uniform conceals an exquisite assassin. They walk at the mother's side through the flowered alleys of a garden that moment by moment grows darker; they have no idea why the sun disappears or bleeds; why the roses and lilies which at first dappled the carpet of the grass are replaced by horrid briars; why instead of gracious birds, immobile serpents hang from the limbs of the trees; why the gentle words of their companion little by little, as they enter further into the woods, acquire a cruel accent and a frightening meaning. Charmed by that voice, calm and sensitive like no other, guided by that gaze, tender and sinister as but a few, they tremble and stutter queasy words of doubt, of gratitude, of weakness and of horror as they proceed on the mother's arm towards the

House that appears at the back of that tangle of briars, in those mysteriously lighted shadows; and finally we see— but we can no longer rebel, flee, or even drop that hand— instead of the table, the bed, the fire, and everything else so tenderly hoped for, we finally see the solitary gallows that awaits us: the gallows to which the person we love will accompany us. And after so much suffering, so much disquietude, so many tears, you will ascend it docilely, conquered by the kiss, planted with a tenuous sigh, on your cheek.

Perhaps a tear will sparkle in the eye of the marvelous friend as the rope reddens the victim's throat; he may finally feel some tarnished form of pity.

For anyone whose life is entirely entrusted to the whim of another—and no matter if that person, belying our fears, counts as one of the finest—there is surely no peace or goodness on this earth. And the terrible noises of war, the redness of blood and the whiteness of water in revolt, the clamor of rivers overrushing their banks and the din of earth ripped apart by quakes and convulsions, neither any of that nor the falling of mountains and the flaming death of stars, nor the wreck which a person, an epidemic, or a mob demanding justice might inflict—nothing, truly, is any longer of importance. The sun rises only in the eyes of the beloved, if by chance they smile; all tempests, and every most horrid catastrophe, every most bitter death, lie solely within the circuit of the lover's own forehead, if by chance those eyes fall upon it, indifferently, with a cold sidelong glance.

Fhela and the Melancholy Light

The evening I first encountered my Light—the first as well that I passed in this tower—was one of untold wonder.

I found myself, initially, at the back of the room of the Great Winds, of which terrifying things were said, but now they were not there. Before me far in the distance stood an open window; and scudding golden clouds beyond, reflecting for a moment in the panes of glass, then gone, followed by others less bright. No plant yet held its place beyond the window sill. No Lady of Pain paced before it. There was no flux of coursing lights: the window opened onto great grey-blue quiet and those pliant, ever-dimmer clouds. I felt inside me nothing but blankness, before that sudden joy. I was in fact close to sleep when the moon appeared. In an instant she had risen to the Mountain's bluish ridge and quickly untrussed her splendid hair, shaking it out in the sea. In her wake a doleful sweetness pervaded the room's darkness, the walls swelling forward towards the light. The waters of the bay lamented, and likewise scattered long white hair along the sea-wall steps. Half sitting up in my bed, I flushed with amazement: at the sight of the moon no less than of the thousands of eyes that turned here and there to observe her. Yet hardly more than an instant passed before she slowed, blanching from the speed of her flight, and reclined against the sky, lifting her forehead almost as though to weep. "Do not look at me," she said. I too obeyed, and—suddenly, a mystery—a numberless string of lights appeared: all along the Mountain, as well as here below.

Their attention, rather than focused on the moon, was turned quite fixedly to me, without so much as an eyeblink. I slightly trembled from the spell of it, and as well from a strong desire to hide my face in my arms. But in fact (partly too from a sense of decorum) I couldn't.

Suddenly I implored, "Please don't look so hard." But the words resounded only in my mind and the Lights continued to watch me. I could feel the touch of their eyes.

Then, when after a time it seemed that movement would give no offense, I went to the other window, which directly faced the first from across the corner. It was shut: during those days of my approach from across the sea a demonic display of the Winds had blown in, full of dances and chants.

Though sheltered by the window's glass, I saw myself observed by other pale Lights beyond, each one peering from its balcony. Perhaps they were out for a breath of air. Above them were great black roofs and steep declivities, and monstrous hints of terraces with sheets that for a moment raised their arms in defiance, and then fled. Still higher up was the darkness of the Hill, with trees of a similar darkness, and a few other Lights, somehow astray. Five sat in a circle, I could see them, and they watched me. There was nothing else for them to do. Perhaps they discussed me. I felt very much unhinged, and directed my gaze beyond them, up to the Hill's chaste profile in the dark tranquility of the sky. A number of youthful pines, one behind the other, chased gracefully along the crest, blue tracery showing through their hair. (Running in innocence, just as ever afterwards.)

Comforted slightly by these dancing trees, I almost smiled; but my distress quickly returned. There on the Hillside's furthest slope, where houses began, was a Light, blond and large in the greenish evening sky, and boldly observant. Fairly more transparent than the others, he had an air not of pain but of something bemused and inward, resembling a person (the image occurred to me later) so fully aware of his own interior frailty and lack of worth as to find it beneath mention. That melancholy parted my lips— out of admiration, yet also from knowing myself to be watched. I averted my eyes automatically, momentarily, to the shining abyss that was the moon. I looked away so as not to see him. But then I looked back: his gaze is supremely magical, and cannot be denied.

What is he thinking? What can he want? His eyes continued to study me with calm and outright tenderness, as if I were his possible salvation, or a mooring in time—as though aware and yet careless of how bitterly ludicrous it would be to harbor futile hopes; aware of the impossibility, in so low a state, of finding a home in my thoughts. I'll say no more. I raised a hand to my face and listened to the plaint of the waters, to the endless curiosity of the Lights running to larboard on their boats—the better to see me. Through half-closed fingers and the mirror of a tear, I glimpsed that calm and wholly tranquil Light as he rested his chin on a roof and widened his eyes still further, survey-ing me constantly.

I can give no account of my tormented night. I had seen this tower as the place in which to live out my life, and coming to it I imagined at last to find solitude. But now, instead, I find myself at the focus of a world, with those who watch me, others who guard me, others who love me. More than anything else, that glimmer of possible friendship kept me awake with the shadow of a laugh on my lips (pondering how low I had fallen) and yet with a heart that brimmed with youthful exuberance.

Towards midnight I heard first a scraping, as though someone were attempting to force the window, laughing while cutting a hole in a pane of glass. I pulled my head beneath the sheets and shut my eyes in alarm. It was the Wind. The wind had always frightened me, while also awakening a cautious empathy. Rather like the feelings—I lack a clearer phrase—that a thief might arouse. But now I made out, in the laughter of the wind, a vague tone of ridicule, which in my current state of mind set my heart racing. And as I listened to the wind, I attempted to imagine that my Light was far away, and to see all the things I have mentioned as an unaccustomed dream. Why not simply ignore him? He was a stranger I had never seen before. Or I could offer some utterly small greeting. But that was surely the last thing to do. Better to show no interest at all. He was destitute and foreign. I struggled to defy an inexplicable feeling of tenderness, an emotion of painful, heart-felt commitment he had somehow aroused. Again the wind laughed slightly, and left. Sleep was impossible, even at that late hour. I studied the Lights that strolled up and down in the darkness, yellow hats concealing their eyes. Did my mind have truly no other choice than to dwell on that melancholy creature? What was happening to me? The Lights continued their orderly promenade across the panes of glass.

As I began to fall asleep, despite my restless sighs, I heard a powerful *Dong*, and then a rushing of air—almost as though of a person falling. My ears filled with a clear and clamorous voice, which only *seemed* to be a bell. In fact it was a person. *Dong*, it repeated, and recounted an infinity of distant and arcane things, all rehearsing a theme of incitement to action. My heart trembled. The voice rose as though from beside my breast, and I was certain that a huge, veiled woman had come to lay at my flank, confiding her afflictions and then telling me to sleep. *Dong.* Everything she said was spoken with this single word. But when after a while I turned to allow her to weep in my arms, no one was there. What, oh God, had happened? This gentle Woman seemed to have slipped away through the window overlooking the sea, and was singing as she moved into the distance. I realized (though certainty awaited the following day) that she must have been the village Bell, and had come here only for me, to tell me of her trials and tragic destiny. Or did her story recount something else? Her weeping had seemed, inexplicably, to have been for me…as though she were frightened, distraught, or alert to some predicament I faced. Yet I knew that I lived in safety.

I thought, "She'll be back tomorrow, always." But I didn't know why. And the thought that this grandiose woman would return to my side with every dawn—always lavishing vitality and tenderness—prevented me from falling back to sleep. Then I remembered my little friend, how he had gazed in my direction. What will he be doing now? I wanted to spring out of bed and rush to the window to greet him. But a terrible dread that my behavior might seem strange made me halt. That or some other unbearable doubt— perhaps the fear that others might see me. I abandoned myself, with widened eyes and growing trepidation, to deciphering his thoughts and fondly taking the measure of his melancholy—of all the centuries he had not known me, of the feelings I aroused in him now.

The following morning I ran to the window (the one with a view of the Hill), anxious to direct him a greeting, though properly, and also to acknowledge those others who lived in the hillside houses. My pensive friend, no different from the others, had paled in the great dawn light. I stood perfectly still but allowed my eyes to reveal how much he had occupied my thoughts; I held myself motionless since I was afraid of somehow giving offense. He seemed to swell with a mixture of joyous wonder and a plaint; then he advised me to go to the other window (imagining that other lights were about to arrive).

Here I discovered a large strange plant by the name of Fhela. It was as tall as a human being, and it trembled in that early morning light, but I paid it scant attention. The evening's endless sequel of lights had now disappeared, and the sea was calm and dark. Only a single Light remained (it seemed), pushing away at that very moment from the sea-wall steps, aboard a boat. He returned my smile with a nod of the head, and blushed. He had to go out to beyond the Red Houses, and from there he soon returned.

This air of complicity, and especially his blush, made me stiffen, my eyes continuing to follow him while I thought that, yes, he might just as well go off. A sailboat, as he crossed before its prow, gave a brief salute by dipping its forward mast—a movement that might have been ascribed to the rolling of the tide—and the Light of the Boat then quickly disappeared in its lee. Other boats advanced and I studied them closely. Three were old and hoary; one was young and gaily painted; behind them were a number of others asleep in the rosy sea-light, their yards hanging low in nets of gold and drowsiness. On the three older ships were several Lights in hues of gold or blood, reclining in circles or randomly scattered. Seeing me, they at once broke off their tales of pirates and proudly lifted their heads. Flaming just behind them rose the fire of a beautiful Light I had not seen before, owing to his constant pivoting.

He too observed me—fixedly and frankly. Once again flustered, I vehemently turned my head in search of my pensive companion, who, out beyond the other window, resting his chin on a run-down roof, grew pale. I was moved by the fears I guessed him to nourish as he thought of me, so even while intrigued by the roving gazes from out on the sea I was careful to show him my most tender reassurance. Instantly he trusted me, and flickered out.

I determined then to do no more than bask in the morning air, and turned my eyes toward the sea while holding a hand to my heart, as though suppressing the tremor of my newly born affections. What I found most appealing in this friend of mine was his calm and impassioned, while always solemn gaze, his golden head, his composure. I liked the others too, I remarked to myself, but him most of all.

Meanwhile, the Light of the Boat returned, saying "Please" beneath lowered eyes, and the other sailboats moved aside. I felt highly amused no sooner than I saw him, struck perhaps by that bashfulness which diverted his gaze from the faces of others and propelled his boat into rapid flight. I had quickly discarded any notion that his thoughts might dwell on me—he had seen me in the tower, and my graces are slight—so I found no explanation for his charging away so impetuously.

The Red Light regarded him steadily as he passed nearby, and then shifted his eyes in my direction, as though inviting me to share a laugh at him. Once again, those eyes proved capable of wounding me. Though nearly a mile away, he was yet so bright and large and red as to seem to perch on my windowsill. Later, on days of stormy weather, I was to see how tiny women with baleful faces would rise from the sea to embrace him, and how he in turn would

ward them off with laughing scorn. One wouldn't call him
cruel, but his manner was marked by a blithe and startling
brutality; it appealed to me even while increasing my appreciation of my wistful, solitary friend. The thought of my
friend, I realized, had the quality of a tender pain (perhaps
by contrast), almost as though he were less a meager Light
or simple lamp, than a genie, a winged lord. I wished to
think of nothing or no one else, and my mind dwelt only on
his steadfast gaze. The Red Light must have understood,
since he ceased to stare in my direction and conversed in
the great growing dawn with the Corsair Lights who balanced on the masts of the sailing ships. As these thoughts
(or fancies?) revolved in my mind, it seemed that they
spoke of forests, bright red forests! My Plant quivered, but
nothing more; she was quiet and cheerless, as though indifferent. I too shivered as I looked at the silent creature.
A few Lights went out, remarking on the forests' *beauty*.
Others shined more brightly and then went out saying the
same. A *Dong* resounded through the air, but remotely,
and all eyes turned in that direction, believing it to be the
Lady. But the Lady of Pain was nowhere visible. When
after a while the sun appeared, I withdrew into the tower.

What days were now to follow! My thoughts return to
the evening when I saw my Light again, among the others,
and I remember how my mind's pained laughter was drowned
by ecstatic comprehension. Had it not been for the others,
my joy would have been complete.

As soon as the window facing the hill flushed green, I
knelt on the chair before it, expecting my melancholy Light
quite soon to appear. His modesty and gentle desperation
intrigued me; I was curious, too, about myself. Nature (or
Humanity—the most squalid and confused of the pictures
that artists have ever been known to hang on the walls of the

Air) was there to await him. Always that lifeless hill, those cliff-like houses, that laundry more hanged than hung. But when my Favorite suddenly appeared from behind dark eaves, as though having run, and glanced with a smile in my direction, my spirits were gripped by the strongest enchantment. Motionless, I was almost paralyzed. "Is anything wrong?" he repeated. "Is anything wrong?" My gaze answered his own as I propped my arms on the windowsill, still fearing my ironic cast of mind, though trembling already with gratitude and careful to keep such human emotions from showing on my face. I was frightened by the thought of an expression he might find wounding. His happiness knew no limits. He fixed me with a stare of radiant calm and unplumbable affection, yet still (from a certain sober stiffness) as though aware of my hidden frame of mind, or at least of how *different* I was.

This awareness was precisely what drew me towards him. Likewise it made me sad. My situation filled me at first with human trepidation, but the more his eyes observed me, the more I discovered a state of calm. There were no other Lights, not even on the sea, and that, for me, was a comfort. So sweet an evening. The second. (Throughout the day, I had cried and laughed—amidst my sighs—as I had pondered the personal soul.) Now I was able to talk—though I could not hear my voice—and I listed the things around me: lights, boats, a plant. I remember the painful glow of his pallid face as he smiled and asked if my preference did not in truth go to them, rather than to so modest a friend. I passionately replied, "No, no, how can you think such a thing?"

"Isn't there a Red Light?" he enquired darkly.

I replied that there was, and despite my entreaties he said nothing more.

He had such a pained and simple way of holding

silence as to make me smile through my tears. And I was to spill my tears quite frequently from that time forward, after each of our conversations. These are painful things to recount; but that hardly matters.

So in just a few days he was mine, and his fine blond head had a permanent place in my heart, just to the left of the tiny portal of Irony. I loved him desperately for two reasons. The first—almost too obvious for mention—was the wonder and enormous pleasure I found in watching him grow, the growth of his sensibility. The other: I didn't love him alone, even if I cared for no one else in quite the same way.

I had realized just how intensely he enjoyed our friendship, sounding even the darkest delirium (even if innate restraint prevented his showing it, or at least his surrender to happiness.) I knew he had placed his hopes in me alone, even while holding his silence; and no reflection on my nature as a human being would have served to divide us, not even the most unfeeling burst of laughter. Laughter, to be sure, was always abundant. All our visits resounded with the laughter of the wind at my back, and Lights would course on the boats, cavorting in desperate desire, insisting that I love them too, and let them burgeon in my eyes. How might I have done that? Yet they left my feelings in turmoil, bringing me close to tears. I was careful to hide this from my friend, since I could not have borne his pain, but it was hard. On his own he might have noticed their curious gestures, and remarked my own disquiet. The handsome Corsairs indeed knew nothing of bashfulness; they were basically a race of predators, laughing and dancing with broad gesticulations on the sea. By dawn they paled and would enter the rosy port, seeking berths here and there and gazing towards my window to interrogate the beautiful Fhela, who remained closed up within herself and paid them no attention. Then I'd hear again the musical cry of the Lady of Pain, sounding across the pinkish waters, but without assuring my safety. The Corsairs and their stories of bright red forests left me edgy and unnerved. Such melancholy days! But the one who most unsettled me—along, on this particular score, with the Light of the Boat—was the Red Light. I knew him to be the confidant of the Light of the Boat—they shared sleeping quarters—and the Light of the Boat was obsessed with the thought of abducting me. (He would pass quickly by with downcast eyes and a voice of loudly splashing oars.) I knew as well that the Red Light had taken up the bitter habit of covering me with ridicule—jeering at my intimacy with the small and solitary Light who flickered on the hill. Once, while the Red Light attempted to harass me with sarcastic barbs about the vanity of all affection, a wave in the form of a woman rose up with whitish hair and clutched at his feet, to silence him. He dived back into the water and reappeared farther off, between two bobbing houses, and extended his luminous arms. The sea contained compassionate forces, but there was nothing they could do. The Red Light saw only folly in my affection for an abject bead of Glass (as he considered my friend to be), and all the more, he insisted, since I was probably on the verge of marrying him. And so...how could I have told my little friend of my thirst for the others? I could not have made him understand that what intrigued me—especially in those who were most erratic—was precisely their natural barbarism; or that watching them return in the evening on an ancient boat or a great black sailing ship could make me shiver. Or that a strange disquiet could rivet me to endless tales of lost forests, and of suns extinguished in poisonous lagoons.... Such candor would have made him feel betrayed; in the green evening I'd no longer be able to greet him with a smile. Nothing, moreover, could have made me forget the pain of his first experience of joy.

So I suffered. And yet I found no peace except in his company. The religious intuition of primordial absurdity—the sense of Irony—welled up within me, and he would newly, unawares, stand before my eyes as all the more adorable. To see him doubt me, in all his childlike intensity, would wrack me with shocks of wonder, bringing me almost to tears. How could I ever forget him? Or give him up?

Whenever I sensed his disquiet, or watched his pained uncertainty on the limits of human fidelity, an authentic passion would quicken all the more inside me—a passion woven from the saddened awareness my own incapability of devotion. At times—even during the day, when his face was pale or invisible—I wished I might be out in the streets with him. I imagined how he'd stand beside me, blond and thoughtful, and that tears of enchantment would moisten my eyes while I stood within his light. Later, when I'd confess these affectionate follies, he'd laugh his heavy laughter and his face glowed more intensely. But he didn't speak.

"Wouldn't you like that too?" I insisted.

II

Little by little it struck me (though perhaps it was a painful illusion) that voices no longer beckoned from the sea. Something to be happy about. Young Fhela, my plant, meanwhile had budded a flower, pink with golden stamens, and promising to deepen into red. I had never before seen anything quite so fine, and I admired it constantly. It had also been noticed from out on the sea, by the Corsair Lights, the Red Light, and all the others, except for the Light of the

Boat, which, alone, had begun to pass by more frequently. The evening I discovered the flower, I rushed to tell my Favorite, and he too, though with all his usual gravity, began to take an interest in the silent creature.

Fhela I imagine to have come from very far away, yet nothing about her gave hint of any consolation that such distant origins might have afforded her. Imagine a great serenity that gathers in the course of the day and then with approaching evening lapses into a tremor. When I observed her from a distance—from the back of the room—she stood there grand and luxuriant against the windowed wall while water moved between her leaves, water and passing lights. She seemed swollen with light and melancholy: a stupendous ripeness, an anxiety while waiting for I couldn't say what. Whenever I approached, I could feel her retreat, almost imperceptibly, her breathing growing husky, as though faining not to show herself, or not to speak. She drank light. We had a number of evenings of fine spring weather, and there were ever more hours when I sat beside her, never addressing her and as though not seeing her, looking out through the other window at my friend. I was at peace. A golden cloud would come, or another no less gold, and would graze against Fhela's leaves, which would blush, or against my cheek. Then other clouds would come, always larger, and we seemed to navigate in brightness. These were moments of sheer beatitude. I didn't find it hard to fathom her state of mind, the ease with which she'd weep when a wayward breath would pass, that marvelous vision which surely always stood before her thoughts, making her silent and recondite. One evening when the sky was crowded with golden clouds reclining in festive conversation (hugging green mantles to their breasts and slowly undoing their hair), I approached her and playfully rested my head among her leaves. A tiny branch prodded against my chin; I felt a leaf against the lid of my eye; and Fhela imperceptibly withdrew into herself. I was overtaken by a secret misgiving since the odor I caught was acrid and sweet, and a quiver was passing among the leaves, the beginnings of a great, unspoken word. I moved away, Fhela trembled silently, and I saw my friend before me. He sadly nodded and lowered his head, in reproof of my lack of feeling. But he did not speak.

I was taken aback and again rested my head among those leaves, and again felt a twinge of anguish upon perceiving that unavowed word. A Light, meanwhile, arrived from the sea. Then another, then many. They rose to their feet on their boats and stared in our direction. The moon dipped a finger into the water to see if it was cold, before descending. "We see, we see, we see," they all cried feverishly. A few of the Boats turned around to look.

My white Light did not move. I saw how he ever so slightly inclined his head to survey me more clearly, and that kindly gesture went straight to my heart. In the great pale evening, near to my plant, I was truly happy.

How then could that Storm blow in and banish him from my mind, if only for a very few hours? Yet long enough to swamp him with anguished awareness of his poverty. But now I'm to tell how this tempest arrived, and exactly how desperate it made me. How, as well, I could save myself, thanks to a Woman's kindly visit, then, once again quieted, to resume my life with my Friend.

I had told him, "Tomorrow, I'll come earlier," and then I had gone to say good-night to the Corsair Lights at the other window. It was already late and time to retire. But I had barely approached the window panes when a violent moan resounded, a great thud, and then nothing more. The Wind! Immediately afterwards several boats with Lights charged by at enormous speed, sounding with gusts of laughter. I waited in avid astonishment. Time slipped past without the return of that great dull thud, that sinister burst of hilarity, and I was certain it had to be heard again. Yet it wasn't. The Red Light appeared, as though speaking from out in the open sea, with reports of billowing clouds. He struck me as extremely content with himself, widening his single fiery eye. Rising and descending again and again through the rigging and the lines of the sailing ships, the Corsair Lights inspected the horizon. They seemed maddened by fever and talked of the winds—who knows how many and how strong they were! The Light of the Boat, during a span of much confusion, made his way to the Red Light's side and confided his secret afflictions; it was then that the Red Light noted my presence at the window of the tower. Savagely derisive, he stared quite fixedly. The Light of the Boat then turned as well to look in my direction, his dark smile charged with his entire grief.

"Why do the two of your stare at me?" I said to the Red Light.

"You'll see, you'll see," he replied, wildly fluttering his eye.

Long black waves came to beat against the harbor steps, attempting to climb them, but failing, and then drawing backwards with foam at their lips. Here and there the sea filled up with ghostly women.

Nothing, however, was yet to take place in the course of that night, and my fears took comfort in illusions of peace, even though a darkness paced back and forth across my heart. But who was to arrive...or what?

It was nearly six o'clock on the following evening (I had already placed my chair by the western window, where I'd sit to talk with my friend) when a number of clouds, bristling with tatters and huge as hills, in fact scudded down from the Hill and without so much as halting to mirror themselves in the black panes of glass announced that the hour had come: the Winds' arrival. And in the very same instant in which this news arrived, small white horses appeared on the sea, allowing the Lights to leap into saddle and gallop full force into the bay. The moon too had issued from her sheets and was dragging them behind her, running rosy through all that silver to look for safety among the clouds, emerging from one to go into another: a fearful sight. And great Green Mountains now loomed up behind the clouds!

I watched my Corsair Lights as they climbed the masts of the sailboats to observe the storm, drunkenly swaying their heads. Aging schooners slipped their moorings and murmured amongst themselves and dipped and bowed in the pleasure of the fury. Wings of snow, gulls perhaps, fled here and there in the dark, trembling as they sought the Lights, so then to be able to settle on the Boats. The sea, in all this darkness, was aflutter with red Lights and white gulls. A tall black schooner quickly entered, and then a boat with a single sail, square and reddish purple, tall as the sky, with some twenty Corsairs crouched at its pinnacle. As cries sounded through the air, another turned to say, "Have no fear, and trust me," but small white horses leaped to its back to kick and prod it along. If a Light was in the saddle, it would bow and doff its hat. Howls in the air grew ever more numerous, from I couldn't say what direction. I felt compelled to close both windows, but not the shutters: Fhela and my Light, if unable to see me, might have trembled in terror and apprehension.

FHELA AND THE MELANCHOLY LIGHT

*   *   *

But in fact they were not afraid, neither the one nor the other, or they refused to let it show. The eyes of my luckless friend, who rested his chin on the eaves of a roof while peering towards the tower, remained steady and serene; my silent plant didn't look at me at all. She slightly flushed and swelled. Leaning forward to the purple abyss, the frenzied moon passing through her hair, she seemed self-absorbed. Again, for the very first time since that first evening of fleeting clouds, I saw that she was moved: a nameless commotion made her tremble, even while enclosed in her accustomed reserve. She seemed to have reached some summit of maturity and to await who knows what miracle. It seemed ready to erupt from inside of her: she'd turn into a forest and grow bright with bird-song. I wanted to open the window and touch her, to say "Let's wait together." But I could not. I remained behind the panes of glass, and felt myself grow little by little more anxious and annoyed with the friend who at my back surveyed me through the other window. Why did he have to stare? I wanted my Corsairs, I wanted to study the Winds. I couldn't perhaps insist that my fever received no assistance from the Red Light's haughty gaze—which nearly suggested that I acquiesce to the baseness of his comrade's will—but I also knew it to originate in Fhela's silent presence and her overflowing beauty: in what she was seeing—while uttering never a word—within her secret dream. The Winds! The Winds! My thirst for the Winds surged up rapidly from the depths of my fear, and already I was thinking, despite the threats and formidable rebukes that I turned against myself, that now I would draw the shutters of the window towards the Hill when suddenly they descended—pale and tall, with open jaws and leaves in their hair—and the room of my tower began to sway, caught up in their powerful arms. It bobbed up and down like a boat, and the windows clattered in a fearful effort to open themselves and flee from the winds' playful mastery, even calling out to me for help. I rushed to obey—asking in truth for nothing else—and from skies of enormous height the winds thus DROPPED into my room, each of them coursing one behind one another, in and out, a single furious circuit, and singing of FORESTS, FORESTS, RED FORESTS! My tower was full of green mantles. I was standing beside my Plant and gripped my wrists with a force that ought to have snapped them, when suddenly I was in their midst—in the midst of the Winds. I could see how the Red Light glowed with joy—pushing aside a host of women who had risen from the blackness of the sea—and how he turned to call the handsome Corsairs, declaring that the time had come. I was now to depart!

"Yes, yes, yes," whistled the zephyrs and trade winds, the eddying gales and northern typhoons, tearing away their cloaks of leaves and water and releasing their airy, livid, purple throats.

Once within the arms of these gentle creatures—who were tall and very fleet—I understood with limitless joy and amazement what the Red Light's words had meant. Just beyond the windowsill was a great red plain as far as my eyes could reach, with forests too that were red. As I moved slightly forward for a wider view, the trees extended their arms towards the green of the sky; the grasses sang and lay down long against the ground, or quickly stood and ran as a people towards the distant horizon; RED CLOUDS tripped among the fronds and were pulled below with enormous laughter, strands and scraps of them remaining to hang stupefied in the air. This great primitive chorus was joined by the voice of the sea, which came gently to lay its head and arms, all white, on the bosom of the earth. It sang with childlike happiness.

FHELA AND THE MELANCHOLY LIGHT

* * *

But I had wanted from the very first moment to call for someone's aid, and to wrest myself from these gentle creatures' embrace, these eddies and forces of the Air, away from their unendurable joy. "You see my Light," I insisted, "he's calling me, let me go to my Light!" Every time I passed before him—and this was the source of my tribulation—he would press his face against the glazing of the window, as though from a pain that could know no comfort, from the desperate affection I inspired in him. His deep, mute gaze would be the end of me. And before too long the scarlet forest disappeared, together with the crimson earth and clouds: again I saw the sea as it was, black and tearful. I closed my eyes from exhaustion, allowing the winds to pass cool hands across my face, and to scream in my ears with human words of tempest, words that concluded in laughter. They closed in a circle around me, and while leaping up and down sang somber, barbarous songs—all of such great beauty that I seemed from time to time, dulled as I was, to feel the brush of a cluster of bright red boughs (as in the songs themselves) against my face. A frightening delight, and again I clutched my wrists. "Tomorrow," I said, as they whistled and rushed away, "...please. Come back tomorrow." Then I was at peace. It was as though I had returned from a tearful dream, and no further fury was visible. Whole populations of lights were once again on the window panes, my Plant stood firm and ever more florid. A fine three-hued rainbow—blue, white and pale green— rode away, astride the dark sea, to who knows where. A *Dong* resounded in the air, along with the crying of water on the sea-wall steps.

Night now came, and in my bed in the corner of the tower I wept throughout the whole of it, even if quietly. I

55

had made my decision. I would depart, even though every thought of the friend to whom I'd soon be forced to say farewell was also a thought of beseeching forgiveness, as everything within me thirsted to do. What now would his life amount to? In whom would he confide? Without me, he would die. Yet I had to go. My place on the following evening would be off among the migrant clouds, far away from these windows. Yes, the whole of our shared experience stood still before my mind, and I knew how delicate a friendship I had entered; but the fever, I repeat, was great, and I had to go.

In the midst of these thoughts there were moments when I managed to feel more serene, moments when I watched the lights calling out to me: no longer the handsome Corsairs, but the whole of a prayerful people that curved down over the waters, saying, "Come, come, come."

The Red Light too rose up to peer inside, and then threw himself prone on the waters and trembled like a jet of blood, again intoning "Come, come, come," but with a force that revived and doubled my tears. As they all curved forward, the Light of the Boat sped by, back and forth, his head held low as he beat his oars on the water. He was telling me that the time had come, that he intended to carry me off, far away, to a place no longer of towers and calm, and that he asked my forgiveness for his fury; it was simply to save me. Yes, yes, I would go. But how had this all come about? Pained, I turned my face to the wall.

Nothing was to change for several hours.... I remained with my face toward the wall, abandoning all resistance, my mind simply fixed on its own terrors, affections and desperation. Yet then, quite suddenly, the room filled with a glorious lamentation, and a powerful flourish sounded in the air as though a lady had now arrived and was choosing her place. My eyes remained shut, but I knew who it had to be. It was the Lady of Pain of that very first night—the Lady of Pain who had never returned until now. Her voice resounded in all its harmony, and she bent down above me in a single solemn motion. Staring into darkness, I imagined her splendid, widened eyes. She leaned forward and sang. Then she leaned backwards, shaking her mournful hair, and spread her arms. A few moments later they encircled me.

The power of this Lady of Pain is overwhelming, and I began to feel faint. The words of her song were vibrant with wonder and tenderness, as though showing me all of her pity, all of her hope to heal me, as though I were very unwell and needed the strength of her arms if Death were not to embark me on his tiny boat.

"No, no...what, dear lady, are you doing...what are you trying to do?" I muttered breathless questions that she stifled against her breast, holding and embracing me, revealing herself as the world's one Night. And on finding myself enclosed within her arms, there seemed at once to stand before me my friend from the Hill, the friend who had suffered so much on my account, and I longed passionately for his company: to see his face, to tell him of my great repentance, to tell him I would never again abandon my window and our loving conversations, nor entrust myself to the joy of the storms. Shaking with fever, I burned to escape from the arms of the Lady of Pain and to throw myself towards the sill of that window that frames the hill. Foreseeing all the joy I could offer my ill-fated Light, I found myself delirious.

"Let me go, my Lady," I said, "please let me go. Otherwise he will die."

The Lady laughed. Then, holding an arm about my

neck, she led me to the window. We rediscovered the moon, reclining on the hill, aged by the pain she had seen my Friend to suffer. He himself stood as firmly as ever, but with his fine head of gold bowed forward. He didn't see me.

"My friend, my friend," I called violently, "forgive me, I don't intend to leave. Lift your lovely head as a sign of forgiveness. If you cannot forgive me, if you die, I too will perish." Tears streamed down my face.

Two or three minutes were to pass, no more, and Head of Light (a name I sometimes gave my melancholy friend) finally lifted his well-shaped brow. To try to recount that moment would be torture. I know that instants later I threw myself with outspread arms on the windowsill, resting my face against them, and my friend's bright head was beside me. I was safe, free from further terror.

The fine evenings we had known before returned, but were of endlessly greater calm, an ample curtain having dropped on my somber folly with the Winds, on all the Lights, and all the aliens. Now I sat only by the window that viewed the Hill, delighting in it alone, and in the friend who would come so quickly to greet me, who smiled and plied me with questions, and the pain of whose love for me was so intense. Behind me, yes, at the other window, I intuited a great rose-colored glow, and I knew it to harbor impassioned faces riveted to the table of the sea. And, yes, I could likewise intuit the Clouds racing high above, the women at the feet of the Light, the gusts of wind, the handsome Brigands who observed me. But they were no longer of any interest. I was now again untroubled, and there was nowhere I wanted to go. It was enough to be here where I was, with the one small creature I adored. Every trace of irony vanished from my way of regarding him; my only concern with irony lay in watching for its possible presence in his attitude to me. To have found it would have crippled me. If he harbored such a feeling, he never revealed it, possessing the finer irony of compassion. I was always grateful to him. I was happy.

Only one thing saddened me, which was the death of my Silent Plant.

Truly, however, she wasn't really dead; it was simply that I no longer saw her. At dusk one day, a day like any other, I had decided to return to those panes of glass overlooking the sea, where so many lights had passed, and I searched for her. "Pardon me," I spoke with lowered eyes to the Lights, "but where is my lovely Fhela, where is she?" My friend stood before me, and he too was curious. Searching, I discovered in the earth a thin black finger which pointed out a small, yellow leaf, higher up, and I noticed a delicate tremble that shook these poor remains, a sign of their wish to remain unobserved. But I looked at them all the same, quite cordially, and I also leaned forward to touch them with my brow, wanting them once again to remember the wonderful days of a past that now was over and finished. In my heart, I even invoked the splendid winds of the West, asking that Fhela's remains might once again breathe and experience joy.

I recall that I shivered slightly as I called them. They did not come. My friend and I inquired of this lovable creature, and of the others as well, as to what that storm had been. And we shuddered to remember our own.

"There was no such thing," said the Moon.

She was seated on the Mountain with her face aflame, and presented her profile as she looked into the sea. It was a gorgeous, grey, but soundless evening. Two or three Lights passed by in their boats, holding their heads in their hands.

Donat

Early one evening in T——, just before Christmas, I found myself in a room for which I hadn't yet paid the rent, and truly it was one of the coldest small rooms anywhere on earth. It was six o'clock in the afternoon, and rain outside fell uninterrupted, with a grave, secret seething varied only by the wheeze of the wind, which managed, I don't know how, to slip beneath the door and lay cold hands on my feet. That feeling of cold was truly disagreeable. But even less joyful—thoroughly despondent—was the sight of this room where the light was dying, since it was six o'clock, in winter, in the afternoon. The bed was as hard and wretched as a plank, its green-black blanket scrupulously ironed and tucked beneath the mattress along with the edges of the sheets, which were heavy, coarse, rust-spotted linen. And the floor, the walls? Yellow tiles with a black arabesque, very worn and faded; brownish paper with moisture stains. And the window—was the window perhaps more bright? At six o'clock in the evening, especially in winter, a window like this, deep as an embrasure and narrow as a crack in a putrid wall, quite truly suggests no consolation, not to any-one. That's how it was. And that was the reason, this after-noon, finding myself confined to my room and awaiting the arrival of absolutely no one at all, after a day of hearing no voice but the wind…that was the reason, alone in my room, just towards six o'clock, faced with so naked and cheerless a bed, my feet frozen by the wind…that was reason for my feeling such a deep, mounting, and anguished sense of ill-being, even though I could not say if I had been truly aware of it. Perhaps owing to the cold, really I can't be sure, or perhaps to a sip of brandy on an empty stomach, my mind was dull and slightly muddled, not really awake: a torpor left me quite incapable of any decision at all about the cruelty of that pavement, that bed, that window and the room's very walls. I could not destroy them, I could not even dismiss them with a wave of my hand, since it was six o' clock in the afternoon, on an afternoon of unrelenting rain and wind. If this sad little room had vanished, would the rain and wind perhaps have followed? That is the question I could not resolve, and that was why I restricted myself, behind a vague and pointless smile and with sense-less, illogical reasonings, simply to deflecting the distress that was taking control of my thoughts. "It is six o'clock in the afternoon," I said to myself. "Which is a very lovely hour. In other countries, when it's six in the afternoon, in the fall as well as the spring, in winter no less than summer, the sea spreads out like a vast pink cloth, barely striped with blue, perfectly calm and transparent at the edge of the village beach. The houses blush with pink; their balconies are built of strong black wood; and on the windowsills shine velvet stalks of geraniums, as red and bright as paint among the green of their leaves. Light waxes and fails; silence absconds and returns, when it is six o'clock in the after-noon. At six o' clock in the afternoon, a lamp flicks on here and there in the window of a room, illuminating people who sit or move in silence. Boys, resembling so many birds, still run through the squares, but slowly grow more listless. Then, standing in doorways and dressed in black sweaters and red caps, old fishermen appear, blue pants rolled at the cuff. They smoke their yellow-stemmed pipes while watching the unruffled sea, and the sunset that promises a fine tomorrow. All sorts of things can happen at six in the afternoon." And at this further repetition of that mean, sweet phrase, "six o'clock in the afternoon," I began to tremble. I didn't say it any more.

By now it was dark, since it was six in the afternoon, and the force of the rain had doubled. I no longer noticed the troublesome bed, nor that miserable flooring of cold tiles, nor the walls. I saw only the window, as a hazy brightness, and then little by little saw nothing at all. Except perhaps my tears, because it was six in the afternoon.

"At six o'clock in the afternoon, in the summer, naturally, one doesn't much like to turn on the lights," said Donat. Donat was one of my brother's friends and had brushed against my side while making his way to the window.

"In the *summer*. But this, you know, is a winter evening," I faintly replied, just barely glancing at Donat, since my mind was truly terrified of seeing him disappear again. He had entered so very easily!

"Me? Not at all, I don't know anything," replied Donat with that tone of secrecy that rendered his voice so familiar and *unique*. He slightly shifted the curtain at the window (the room had somewhat changed, in place of the bed stood a sofa, merry little paintings hung upon the wall, there was a fine clock and there were painted glasses, and easy chairs upholstered in red velvet; all of it was quite cheerful), and I saw that the sky outside had cleared. The weather, in fact, had never been bad at all. A fullness of light, half red, half golden, flooded that sky, the way it always is in summer at six in the afternoon.

"You never know anything, do you?" I replied, quite happy with that sky and with Donat who had announced it. "You don't even know how long I've been waiting for you. I was upset...I, well, I had dreamed an unhappy dream just before...just before you came in."

"What dream?" asked Donat with a quiet laugh, not bothering to turn around.

"That it was six o'clock in the afternoon. Many years had slipped away, so many, and with a suddenness we could never have imagined. This house had long been empty, the courtyard was deserted, this courtyard you've crossed so very many times on May evenings, wading through a river of moonlight...and the door was closed and hadn't been opened for years, this door you've entered so often wearing your suit of black velvet and bearing your bright black eyes, and a smile. None of this silent joy I feel was any longer right or true, *everything had been*, and was over and done with, Donat, and six o'clock in the afternoon was as vacant as an empty picture frame. You no longer returned, and no longer remembered me. You had grown surly and indifferent. Nor did I remember you. I was in T____, in a freezing room, it was six o'clock in the afternoon, some evening just before Christmas, and it was terrible, because I wasn't expecting anyone, not at that hour, and outside it rained and rained."

"You've always been such a dreamer!" Donat observed rather vaguely. He turned around, his face no longer happy.

"But now I know that all of that was wrong!" I continued, excited and joyful. "It isn't winter, many years have not slipped by, and you, Donat, have not disappeared. That solitude, the rain, the wind that flushed the room with distress at six o'clock in the afternoon—I had only dreamed these things. You're here, you've returned, I'm standing here now before your eyes, and I am so very happy, Donat."

"You've always been such a dreamer," he repeated, coming to sit beside me.

His presence, and above all else the tone of something secret and faintly melancholy in his voice, excited me. As always. I felt that I would give my life if only time would stop, enclosing forever his grave young voice and my no less youthful commotion in this six o'clock in the afternoon, encasing them as though within a pearl. I loved him, and this alone was important: that Donat existed, that he should walk across the courtyard at six in the afternoon and push open the door flooded with moonlight.

I grasped his hand to bring it to my lips.

"It's a lucky thing you never drink," continued Donat ambiguously, without lifting his head to look at me. "I mean, nothing alcoholic."

"What makes you say a thing like that? Of course I don't!" I replied, my cheek against his hand.

"I dreamed tonight...I had the impression..." Donat continued hesitantly. "Any number of years had passed, it was winter, and at six in the afternoon you madly whirled into a bar and were spending your money, and then you saw me again...you saw us again together...."

"But that's not true," I cried, and shuddered.

"Not now...not here...not at this time," Donat sadly demurred.

He put an arm around my shoulder, and that tender, sad gesture brought me against his heart, vainly promising defense against time and the places, pains, and humiliations that announce and follow the hour of six o'clock in the afternoon. I cried warm familiar tears. "But Donat," I said, "you'll always come at six in the afternoon? You'll always come, all the same, even in a thousand years, when this earth will be a place we've forgotten?"

"At six in the afternoon? Yes, of course."

So, after Donat was gone, and even though I saw that I had returned to that tiny room, and even though I understood that the savage clarity of the rain, falling upon the hour of six in the afternoon, just barely illumined my pallid face and apprehensive brow, I felt a light, timid warmth spread through my chest, which was not the effect of a sip of brandy but of Donat's arm around my shoulder—and where had he gone? in what foreign lands was he living, now tired and hardened?—and of his sweet, grave promise, which ever since has always held true, both in tender summer and desolate winter—always—at six o'clock in the afternoon.

Winter Voyage

Usually, when I am able to travel at all, I prefer wintertime. Summer and spring, when the weather is fine, and the early part of the fall, strike me as impossible seasons, what with the light, the heat, and the friendly face that nature turns to mankind, inviting us to stay outdoors. Observing human beings grows ever less reassuring, not because men are evil—quite the contrary—but thanks to that craving for affirmation, that agitation which they carry about inside themselves, that tireless greed which leads them to attack, wound, devour, destroy or simply subdue every living, joyous or dignified thing they meet along their path. Life, clearly enough, demands a struggle; but couldn't that struggle take place with greater understanding for the sometimes weak and voiceless lives of others? That's the question I ask myself.

that's Ortese

There's also something more than the risk, when the weather is fine, of seeing flashes and hearing reports of guns, of encountering hunters with game-bags charged with blood and sky. Fine weather in itself discourages travel. Nature in full splendor is strangely lame; its glory contains some indefinable absence. To return to it can often resemble an older person's attempt to dress in childish clothes: we feel a shiver of unconscious anxiety which we easily mistake for mirth. I dislike such confusions. So when between one snowfall and another the season of fine weather announces itself (you see it in certain lights on the snow, in particular flashes of gold on ice) it strikes me that nothing is better than to close yourself up in your house—if you have one—with a pile of books, locking the doors and windows and patiently waiting first for *the season of the flowers* and then the harvest to tire themselves out. Unfortunately, for the past few years, these seasons last ever longer. The rains never arrive, not even storms; snow is scarcer than happiness. There's only a bare, harsh sun that makes life seem even more alarming than it is; alarming, and, I dare to say, absurd. But now that winter has finally come, it's better not to recall the sad days of May. One has to learn, after all, to appreciate things in the moment in which they offer themselves, without thinking too much about when they'll again disappear.

I'd like to tell the story of one of these winter voyages—one of these trips in the season I love so much and so keenly anticipate. I had kept on the brakes, as the saying goes, until the beginning of January, waiting for the end of the so-called *holidays*, which really round down to a kind of artificial summer. But after the Feast of the Forty Martyrs, on January 7, I could hold out no longer. The city's stores were already plying little packets of streamers and enormous red noses; and after quickly dispensing with fir trees and all their merry lights, people talked only of costumes and cotillions. I could see that putting things off for a few more days would have meant to risk encountering a new explosion of civil life. I had to leave at once! So, on the evening of January 8, a Sunday, I made my way to the station. I set out when the hour was already late, nearly night, to avoid the possibility of a crowd. But my worries were quite unfounded: the bad weather (a dark, gelid sky and a few first scatterings of snow, mixed with rain) had counselled even the most intrepid citizens to remain at home, and rush hour workers' traffic was long since over. What an ugly, wonderful night! I was wearing my very worst clothes, the most worn out; the ones, I'd say, most consecrated by poverty and bad taste. Nothing special, if you like: a dark green coat, enlivened by a pattern of small red squares; high-laced shoes for the country; a gray wool beret, surmounted by a white wool scarf sporting decorative little garlands of flowers; hairy grey wool gloves that revealed chapped, red fingertips. And finally an umbrella of green, waxed canvas, tattered and terribly antiquated, and a small cardboard suitcase in which I had placed no more than a shawl from a neighborhood market, purchased quite cheaply, and a couple of handkerchiefs. My poverty, even without being exemplary, filled me with a kind of savage joy, a voluptuous cast of mind I would find it difficult to explain. Let's put it like this: I stood outside of our era of grandiosity, outside of these miserable times of formidable objects abundantly produced by industry. Nothing, I had nothing.... I was free! I wasn't planning to go very far: I'd travel across the Piedmont plain and intended to go as far as the sea, so as to watch it from some old café in a city near the border. On certain rainy afternoons or evenings, it is very beautiful to watch the sea from a seat behind the window panes of a little café in a city or village along the frontier. In that atmosphere of boredom, such a boredom! And such a din! And the sea, with all that foam! How huge it is, how useless and alone! Such a contrast to the very few people who cross the square, to this one or that one who sits in the quietest corner of the old-fashioned room, people who don't seem useless at all. Or perhaps they do, but at the end of a history that hasn't been useless or in any way vulgar. I find that people who have known no worldly success are always fascinating. People who already have nearly slipped off the edges of the screen of life, and then who stop there, beneath some final sun, show such clear outlines, a true nobility, such sparkling gentle eyes. Who knows if I'll be able to say exactly what I think? (But perhaps *exactly* is not at all *the way* I think, and there you have it.)

In short, I had boarded a train. I had purchased a third class ticket (as good a way as any for avoiding vulgar company) and I found myself content. I travelled all night long, delighting in the cold which despite my various expedients—and owing perhaps to a breakdown in the electrical system (or, more probably, to my imagination)—took penetrating charge of that tiny, solitary, mobile room. At eight o'clock the following morning—thanks to fog it was still quite dark—we reached a small town not far from Turin. We had slipped past the city as though in a dream, and even had I wanted to, I couldn't have gotten off there. But I wouldn't have wanted to. I am terribly fond of small forgotten cities, of towns reduced to the silence of ancient villages, forgetful of our present days, and that's how this one was. Perhaps because of the cold, of the dismal air, not a soul was to be seen, and the town's only carriage conveyed me to "The Green Cap," an ancient inn at the edge of an orchard, or a garden, or the open countryside; one couldn't really tell, thanks to the thick mantle of snow that lay on top of everything, covering bushes, ditches and trees. The view from my third-floor room (reached by way of a narrow wooden staircase) opened out onto white, uniform solitude. I spent beautiful hours in front of that window, attempting to fathom the wants of certain poor little birds that threw themselves through the air with a cry. I thought.... I asked myself.... But no, I thought absolutely nothing; and I asked myself no questions. Such torments had subsided. At two o'clock, after a light lunch of fried eggs and cole slaw, accompanied by a cold, red apple and a cup of salty coffee (but the stove behind my table crackled in compensation, with red and blue tongues of flame leaping through crowns of golden stars), I again picked up my suitcase and donned my beret. I paid my bill to the hotel keeper and with lively pleasure set out toward the station. I remember how the cold attacked my legs and leapt to my hands to pinch the fingertips left exposed by the holes in my gloves, how it touched my chin and eyes with thousands of silvery needles. My forehead froze completely, my thoughts as well were frozen and beatific, no longer thoughts at all, simply the certainty that this was winter! Back at the station: the train again—the only train on all the tracks; the fog again, thickened by a bit of rain in the morning hours; and that sense of eternal solitude, no longer bleak and rational as we find it in regions blasted by industry, but mindless and entirely tender as we know it in the lands of childhood. The train, practically a freight train, began to move and reached a moderate speed. Other cities and villages went by, mountains rose and receded from view, a stream appeared, flowing beneath a little bridge and flanked by a row of willow trees, and then that too was gone. Towards five o'clock (again it seemed to be night), the light came on, a very tiny lamp, and we began to ascend into the mountains, which really weren't mountains at all, but caverns, then trunks of trees, then blacks and whites as though in a photograph, nothing more—something quite absurd—until finally they ceased to interest me. When I reawakened—since indeed I had fallen asleep, resorting to the remedy I always use when my mind loses all grasp on things—we were up in the mountains or off beyond them, I couldn't say which, but there were people too. I was no longer alone.

These three or four people were the usual lot who cross the plain in the wintertime, laden with packages and paper bags: a man, two women—one of them old—with faces drawn by two or three lines, their eyes reduced to a tiny light, as though fatigued, but ardent and calm, by a question that came and went like the *chug-achug-chug* of the train. I didn't dislike them, but they weren't what aroused my interest.

Seated directly in front of me in the corner by the window (I occupied the compartment's other window seat) was a man—later I learned that he came from Santander— who continually stared at me. He was a young man, perhaps no more than a boy, wrapped up from knees to neck in a black cape such as people have generally ceased to wear, except in certain Iberian villages, and I couldn't say whether he was handsome or homely, refined or vulgar. A poor soul, at first sight, quite lithe and nonchalant, to judge from the way he studied me, since he was otherwise utterly motionless. He looked at me as though he recognized me and were expecting a nod (he was proud) or a salutation, I couldn't quite tell what. And on seeing that I, most certainly, had no such greeting to offer, or would curtly have retorted that, no, I did not know him, his strange, somehow haggard face grew taut, its lips like those of a dog, just barely annoyed and sarcastic. But his blue-green eyes remained serene: rather than annoyance they only showed surprise and seemed a little hurt. "How's that," he appeared to say, "aren't you going to say hello? Did I really mean nothing at all to you?"

And these were not the words that a man addresses to a woman, as such—that was not the situation, and I wouldn't want to talk about such a thing—but to a relative. Or better to a friend. To a companion with whom one had lived through a time of lunar moods and solar insights, sharing bread, laughter, hopes, and more.

This was nothing I might have expected! I have often heard it said, but I have never believed it, that life makes room now and then for encounters that do not belong to life, or to the times in which we live; that it also harbors creatures not logged in any bureau of records. Likewise I have heard it said that not everything we see is real, and that the faces of reality are infinite in number and often remote. And that time is a bridge on which things move in no single direction. And that people can love one another, and lose one another, and then, in the flow of monotonous centuries—as happened when ships were still powered by sail and would re-cross bows an eternity later at the shores of some island—be able again to find and newly to embrace one another. Yet even if such wonders are possible, no such thing could happen to me. I have no recall of other lives; this is my very first existence, and it's not that I find it any too comfortable, perhaps because of the sun, of the violence of its beams, and everybody talks at the top of their voices.

Simply for the fun of it—I had to do something to while away the time—I took out a pencil and a piece of notebook paper and began to sketch a few images, using my suitcase as an inclined plane. The boy across the aisle by the window closely observed my motions. I could see his sorrowful outline, sorrowful and in some way beloved (which of course was impossible), his lustrous eyes, the way he kept the collar of his cape turned up as though to calm the trembling of a fever, like someone ill who crouches up for warmth in the winter cold. He followed my little drawing as it turned into a scene with a window, and beneath the window a laid table, with a petroleum lamp at its center. In Spanish he asked:

"At evening?"

Words, quite clearly, allowing no possible reply, and not only for having been barely whispered. I nodded my head that, yes, that window looked out into evening.

I folded the sheet of paper and set to reflecting on

where I might have seen an evening like the one I now recalled, whether in an old print or in some crease of my personal memory. And suddenly it was no longer winter, nor indeed the odious summer, nor incoherent spring. It was a time altogether of blue cold evenings, on black placid mountains, beneath a sky not brutal, simply high and lively, with clouds that slowly crossed it like great pioneer wagons, puffed up with wind. Then there was a country house, with vast rooms, studded with dark and ominous pieces of furniture. One evening this house grew bright and extraordinary, men and women arrived in black and green, with flowers and guitars, poor people—they had hitched their mules in the courtyard, beneath the light of the moon—and the whole night passed in songs and wine. But I, or someone with me, I really do not know, was sad, since someone else was absent. But that missing person arrived: and he was precisely like this voyager now returning to Santander. A face that was joy itself, showing the very same light as the lanterns. There was great delight, and great light all around.

This reverie was evoked by the lamp, or by the drawing of the lamp, except that I did not know if the person who was sad, and then who was sad no longer, had been myself or someone else. And I did not know if the bond uniting the new arrival and the person who awaited him was of simple blood relationship, or of friendship, or of love. Or if it was a question of two young men; or of a younger and an older person; of a boy and his mother. Or of two friends. The bond between them may even have been political. I repeat, I do not know.

It was time to put an end to such fantasies. I searched for words to address to the young man, and smiled in a banal way, tearing up the drawing. His whole reply, however, was to throw his head to one side, toward our travelling companions, and with a happiness I had never seen in any other person—that's just how resplendent and lively, light and ferocious it was—he set to talking, in a dialect I perfectly understood, about the joy of returning to Santander after a voyage that had lasted…the number of years he said escaped me. And life in Santander was wonderful, just as in the rest of the world, with love, money, and tears: but tears made no difference to him. He mentioned his age—twenty-six—and talked about the fields and houses his family owned in the neighborhood of Santander. They were land-lords: three houses and twenty hectares of ground. He was married, he also said, and recounted the grace of his children.

It seemed as though every happiness he cited were a gunshot fired in the night against a white wall, where some-one stood who could not fall. I found myself reflecting, for the first time, that I myself had nothing, absolutely nothing of what he claimed to have. I was awaited in the city where I lived by a rented room, the bed concealed behind a partition, and a list of bills to pay (but bills for what, since my consumption of life was almost imperceptible?) that never gave me respite. This poverty, which somehow de-fended me from modern life, now made me thoughtful. Yet what afflicted me wasn't so much the contrast between my own meager state and the feast allegedly enjoyed by the voyager from Santander; it was the fact that he wanted to wound me. Why, I asked myself. That intention lay clear in his pale blue eyes.

The compartment's three other travellers nodded in agreement, with that warmth shown by the desperate for the comforts they only know in dreams. The young man, too, was desperate, since clearly his life did not consist of lands, houses, and family, or of the pride of the age of twenty-six. Instead it held poverty and much darkness, and uncer-tainty, as moreover is true for all of us, no matter if his ardor and illusions had once been great. He had the air, for me, of someone who *had reached the end*, and who never again would find it easy to return into *a certain part* of the world.

Yes, now (though always through the play of reflections on the train compartment's window) I too trained my eyes on him, quite openly, and I tirelessly perused the lines of a face which shone with I could not say what depths and reflections of the skies, what spent or dying fire. With some bitter feast; a smile both familiar and obscurely betrayed; a story followed by nothing further. A lament like the voice of the sea, or of a tract of sea swallowed up by a ditch and unwilling to resign itself, wanting to depart anew, but long since trapped.

I suddenly decided—I was weary of so much commiseration—no longer to look at him. So, I too snuggled up into my shawl, which I had taken from my suitcase, and lowered my eyes, where tears were beginning to seethe. The other as well—my son or my friend, who knows what he was?—then suddenly had nothing more to say. With a smile of exhaustion he leaned the whole of his shoulder against the glass of the window, and like a bird fell asleep. But every now and then in his slumber, something passed through him, his shoulders trembled, his eyelashes fluttered—I could see it in the glass—and his beauty, two or three lines, no more, a high forehead, a thin nose, two green-blue eyes, was meek and drained. He as well had the look of someone who had suffered an humiliation, as when over-proud boys come home from school with so many things they want to recount, and their mother who has chores to attend to shoos them away.

So, time slipped by as I sat by the window, remembering and forgetting, remembering and peering beyond it. And suddenly the sea was in view. And even though it was winter, light remained in the air: a touch of something rosy, a vagrant luminosity and a sweetness in the fog, just the way it always is in sea-side towns. Perhaps ten thousand tunnels clattered by, a sun that sank into the sea vanished and reappeared, and the man from Santander, his face turned towards the window, sat forever thinking and dying. And there was nothing for me to say to him—what greater pain?—all the way to the quiet town at the border.

This, I knew, was where I had to disembark, and he would continue throughout the night, towards Cannes, Toulon, Toulouse, such delicate names, in winter. Then one morning in Spain he'd again be in my house—or in *our* house, I imagine—the only house I would have wanted as my destination, but without being recognized, which was why I travelled in winter, and why summer for me contains no meaning or movement. Yet even if this was the only important thing that there remained for me to do, in my life, to go to Santander, it was something I would never do. It was an impossible thing for me to do, and for no good reason— no reason that belongs to this world—it's sad to have to say.

So, as the first houses began to appear—gardens and houses and the lights of the signs of small hotels—rays of light that pricked my eyes like golden needles—I prepared to descend. I would have liked him to get up and to accompany me out into the corridor; but he didn't move, and he didn't speak.

"Good evening to everyone, have a nice trip," I said at that point, politely.

"Have a good stay, thank you, have a good stay, thank you," responded the voices of the other passengers—thin and monotonous like the voices one hears in church: *Kyrie eleison…kyrie eleison….* Only the boy from Santander remained mute, staring at me fixedly through the fingers on which he rested his forehead.

How alone he was, frightened and absent!

I stepped down from the train and turned around, on the pavement, to look at him again. Pretending great delight at having reached my destination, pretending as well to search for the driver of a taxi, I rapidly looked at him once again, and with all the force within my head, a silent force, I cried:

"Farewell, my dearest."

The train was already moving.

"Good-bye my dear...my dear," was the way he answered me.

Whether that was true or only imagined is something I cannot say. A few people now milled about, and life, with its little hotels, its time-tables, its prices—its nothingness— was already resuming.

The Ombras

A house in one of the side streets off Via Tribunali—
Court House Road—was the home, for a while, of one of
those vast and pallid families that live at the edge between
the working and the lower middle classes, struggling to
bring up a swarm of children nourished only on soup and
pasta and housed in large, dark, airless rooms where the
furniture is nothing but odds and ends, just as these people
themselves are the odds and ends of a race. The mother,
Mrs. Eugenia Ombra, brought to mind, perhaps rather more
than the others, that curious entity to which the family
name referred: an *ombra*—a shadow. Which is not at all to
call her a sad or depressed sort of woman, shattered by the
obstinate hostility of Life. Quite the opposite. A deep, fine
smile always brightened her greenish eyes, and she was
kind and affable. But her delicate and somewhat bent little
figure, with her shoulders perennially attempting to punch
through the worn black wool of her dress—and especially
her way of walking when she went to shop, slightly hugging
the walls to avoid being seen, rather as though the sight of
her might represent an offense to the light and to all other
beautiful things existing in the world—quite often made
one think of a shadow. Her husband, Fortunato Ombra, who
for years had run a curio shop near the Ministry of Health,

was now in the habit, owing to an onset of paralysis, of spending most of his time at home; and even though he always loved to dress in the palest of clothes, wearing white linen suits and white cloth shoes even in winter, the impression he conveyed, on closer inspection, was even more marked than in the case of his wife: the impression of being aptly served by their curious surname. He amounted, simply, to a rather white shadow. His green eyes (all the Ombras had large, green, watery eyes) would frequently stare into the distance, assuming an expression that was quite inexplicable.

His sister, Etta Ombra, who had lived with them in that house for over twenty years, was the person, next to Eugenia and Fortunato, who most turned one's thoughts to the realism, greed, and matter-of-factness of small, ordinary people. A chat with Etta was a true delight; she was just that spirited, sharp, and vivacious. But you discovered soon enough that for her too the life of the surrounding world was by no means real. The disappointments and pains she had suffered, which included the death of her retarded and only son, had turned her attention entirely towards Eternity; and since reaching Eternity immediately seemed not to be possible, she compensated, as it were, by savoring a few anticipations. The walls of her room, covered with coffee-colored paper, on which certain little red beasts at times ran silently and unobserved, broadcast a vision of sublime choruses: a thousand images of the Mother of God, the Saints and the Angels, in all possible poses and assuming the most various attitudes: in royal halls and seated amidst the flowers of fine little gardens: here with a mandolin, there with a book bound in red, or with a little white lamb: this one on horseback, that one standing tall on a golden cloud, rosy well-manicured hands extended towards the sky. The rest of the room was fairly humble: a little cast-iron bedstead with a yellow silk coverlet, a dilapidated wash-stand, string curtains grimy from use, and behind the easy chair a window which opened out to that dark marvel, Via Tribunali, that well of suffering humanity. From this room which she kept in order with a kind of jealousy, or with a singular care and affection, Etta Ombra issued every morning at precisely six o'clock, dressed in dignified black; then she scurried down the ample flights of grey, malodorous stairs to the building's heavy front door, crossed the threshold and hurried to the nearby All Souls' Church, where the bells for early mass already had started to ring.

The other Ombras, meaning the children of Eugenia and Fortunato, were not so devout, but still would not have been thought to be mischievous boys and girls. Altogether there were six of them—four boys and two girls—and they differed from one another in only one way. Three of them, despite their tender ages, were as short and stout as wineskins, puffy and white and strengthless; the other three were as long and thin as nails. I was never told why, but all of them, at the time I met them, were dressed in black, and they were always afterwards dressed in black. I imagine the reason to have lain in some ancient mourning, which the price of new wardrobes made it later impossible to abandon. That black attire, while conferring a viscid shine to the former group, gave the latter a nearly transcendent air: their green eyes slipped sometimes into gazes that were full of remote silence and confused visions. Certainly they were quite nice children; but to see them in the evening, towards eight o'clock, around that large, sadly barren dining-room table, one of them intently leafing through a dictionary, another, with a spidery hand, tracing one long thin line on a sheet of paper, while one of the sisters, bent double like a little old woman, was sewing, and another was washing the plates in the sink, her movements just slightly slower than normal and making one imagine a weariness or who knows quite what thoughts—to see them, I was saying, in moments like that would surely have furnished no reason for feelings of peace or euphoria. Eugenia Ombra would sit at such times all huddled up in a corner, her eyes closed, her mouth half-open in a toothless smile, while Fortunato, his own smile obstinate, sat at her side and held his old pipe in a quivering hand. And in Etta's room, further on, one heard a rapid and marvelous mumbling, as though some terribly important visit had just got underway: the widow Etta was chanting her rosary.

I was not so frequent a visitor in the Ombras' house as to have reached an accurate knowledge of the room arrangements, nor indeed, to tell the truth, had I desired to. But I knew nonetheless that in addition to the entrance hall, the dining room, and the three bedrooms, there was also a corridor with a few closets and another smallish room. Yet I would never have imagined that tiny room to have been occupied, or, in short, to contain another Ombra.

I made this discovery quite by accident, and quite painfully as well, since I encountered this other Ombra as that creature was passing away.

Toward the end of an October evening when it rained in the steady and violent way it rains when the world is weary of ecstasies and hopes, the drops of water falling like tears, I found myself in Via Tribunali and decided to seek a few moments' shelter in the home of that kind if slightly dingy family. I was surprised, on reaching their landing, to see their door wide open, with many of the Ombras' family friends freely coming and going, and so distraught as not even to see me.

The strangest thing of all was that *not a single voice* resounded in that house. And yet I could sense that all the

Ombras—father, mother, aunt and children—were present, and just a few steps away.

Suddenly I heard a moan. Quite a singular moan: it resembled the sound of a trickle of water running through high, black mountains, among enormous and impassible obstacles, searching for liberation and the sea. It was much more sad than any simply human sigh.

A door swung open and a white-faced Ombra stepped through the passage, holding a metal basin in her hands, and crying. She didn't see me and continued along her path.

I made my way into the corridor and stopped before another open doorway, out of which spilled a feeble cone of light (the position of the lamp must have been quite elevated), and from there I saw the scene I must now describe.

All the members of the Ombra family, plus two or three other figures I did not recognize, were standing around a bed which was covered only with sheets.

In the middle of that bed, with a lovely pink doll on her knees, sat a creature I had never seen before, but whose image I will always remember.

She couldn't have been more than eight years old, and her body—legs, arms, and belly—was swollen and nearly black. She sat up against a pile of cushions and from time to time, gasping, gave out that weak, fragile, and desperate lament I had heard as I entered.

She too was an Ombra, as I could see from her bright green eyes, and from the black hair that circled her suffering face.

Only much later did someone tell me that Luciana Ombra had been stricken with a heart disease when she was only three years old—the result of some tremendous fright—and that since that time the other Ombras, her relatives, had lavished every attention on her behalf (including that expensive doll). But their bizarre misadventure had also filled them with so great a natural shame and reserve that they were never able to mention it to anyone at all.

In the course of the last few days, quite suddenly, the condition of this young Ombra had taken a serious turn for the worse; and as dusk this evening had fallen, her final agony had begun.

Finding myself, after the rain and the tumult of Via Tribunali, confronted in so desolate a room with a scene of such gravity, not just for the Ombras, but for any human being who chances to witness such a thing, I lapsed into a kind of torpor, due perhaps to the litanies recited by Etta Ombra. Yet in the midst of this trance I was taken aback by the voice of the mother, the good Eugenia Ombra, who every now and then, with the calm timidity of the poor, unshaken by suffering and death, and with a curious smile I can't describe, would say:

"Luciana, this is Mama; what are you seeing now, tell me what you're seeing."

The little girl made no reply, and the aunt volunteered:

"She's seeing angels, ever so many angels...and a wonderful garden."

"Tell me my dear what you're seeing. What are you seeing now?"

And Aunty Ombra: "She sees a lovely palace...and a lady dressed in pink...."

Luciana was breathing very heavily, in a terrible halting way, which perhaps was the reason she couldn't herself reply.

"Leave her alone...now she's seeing God!" said the aged Fortunato Ombra, who stood at the foot of the bed, as he dried away a tear. "Isn't that right, Luciana, that now you're seeing God?"

No reply. The girl's large green eyes, their gaze now nearly cross-eyed, stared fixedly at a point of the ceiling where a large blot of dampness had taken the shape of a picture frame.

"I don't see anything, Daddy," she suddenly remarked with a calm though breaking voice. "All of you are telling me lies."

"*Asperges me hyssopo*.... She's delirious," Aunt Etta remarked with pity, and everyone nodded in agreement.

From among the group, a priest stepped forward with a crucifix and held it up close to the little girl's mouth. I could see that she was quivering like a fish in a net, and everyone rushed to the side of the bed to watch. That was the moment. I could stand it no longer and rushed furiously down the stairs as voices echoed loudly at the end of the corridor, from that gloomy room. "Now she's an angel! She's an angel. Now she's an angel in Heaven!"

The Tenant

More rain, and howling wind. From somewhere in the large room, perhaps from the door, more likely from the window with the broken frame, cold air entered and made the candle flicker constantly. Rather than light, that desperate flame shed darkness on the objects and walls of the room. A huge yellow spider, wholly gold, with four emerald eyes, stared at me fixedly, hanging from the wall before me, up almost at the ceiling. Others, identical though smaller, staggered on their tiny monstrous paws across the pavement and zeroed in on my bed. Grandmother said it was the fever. Seated near the table, where the candle stood, she looked at me from time to time above the rims of her glasses. She was silently at work, mending socks. Suddenly, I could bear it no longer and had to cry out: "Granny! Granny!" I screamed, "They're here now, right up close!..."

I saw her delicate figure, so fine and mysterious, with the short black shawl on her shoulders and the silver keys that tinkled from her belt, rise and approach my bed. Her eyes peered patiently into mine, which were large with fear. With her hand on my forehead, "You've got a fever, that's what's wrong with you...a fever..." she said.

"Granny, send them away.... I'll die if they don't go away!"

Already a spider was running down the covers of the bed. I burst into tears and held trembling onto my grandmother, hiding my face against her shoulder. She cuddled me like that for a while. Then, having firmly made up her mind: "I'll call Mr. Lin."

Mr. Lin was an Angel who lived in her room, and of whom she had always spoken to me as a person of great goodness and extraordinary beauty who spent the day reading, or taking care of injured birds that she herself, Granny, so often found along the road. He was also interested in gardening. Frequently they talked about God and the world, and Granny had told me that at times like that Mr. Lin would grow quite thoughtful. I had never been able to see him, since I didn't believe in him. But on this particular evening, I was so frightened and anxious that anything seemed possible.

Granny went to the door of her room and rapped lightly against the jamb.

"Mr. Lin," she asked, "could you come out for a moment or two? And please bring along that geranium."

A kind voice answered, "But of course I can. Let me first just slip on my jacket."

A moment later the door swung open, and the young man standing on the threshold cut a small but extremely beautiful figure, wearing a roomy, straight-falling jacket in leaf-green velvet. His hair was black and curly, his eyes long and black, vaguely slanted. Eyes that looked like jewels. And his gaze an expression of goodness and infinite calm, perhaps a little sad. In his hand, he held a flowering plant.

Something extraordinary took place at once. The spiders disappeared, and the wind lamenting outside the house in the winter night ceased to moan. The candle flame ceased to fret, and a tranquil light pervaded the room. I felt myself tremble with joy.

"Excuse me," I said, "for having had Granny call you in. I was seeing spiders."

Mr. Lin approached my bed.

"But have you taken your medicine?" he asked, placing a hand on my forehead.

"It's bitter."

"Sit down next to the child for a bit," my grandmother said. "You'll give me a chance to rest. There are so many socks I have to mend."

Mr. Lin put the geranium on the night table, drew up a chair, and then sat down, next to my bed. He was so intensely beautiful, and the meaning of that beauty was a goodness so great that simply by feeling him close to you, you feel a joy such as your heart has never tasted before. Mr. Lin didn't look at me very often, and I could draw from this that up until now I hadn't been a very good girl. There was also that medicine I didn't want to take!

Seeing how I tossed and turned, Mr. Lin said:

"Lie down. Be a good girl."

"It's that I want my medicine," I said.

Granny was about to get up, but Mr. Lin stopped her. He took the medicine, poured out a spoonful, and then put the spoon in my mouth. His hand brushed against my cheek, and I took the chance to kiss it, which he pretended not to notice. Had that annoyed him? I looked at him with true pain and, perhaps I've made a mistake, the faintest of smiles appeared and vanished on his lips.

"Miss Brigida," he said to my grandmother, "do you know what I've discovered? It's that coffee grounds are extremely good for plants. You put on a little every morning. It's the very best fertilizer I know of. This geranium, for example, has flowered again."

"Thanks to all your patience, Mr. Lin," said Granny with a smile.

"Well, I couldn't say. Surely one would try the impossible to help the creatures bloom."

"This morning I read in the newspaper," Granny remarked, "I never buy it, but sometimes it can't be helped, that a revolution has broken out in Bolivia. The President has fled, and many public buildings have been set on fire. I'm worried for those poor people."

For the last several moments, I had been looking at Mr. Lin's shoulders with considerable curiosity. There was not the slightest protuberance. Two smooth shoulders, somewhat frail. No wings at all. He was about to respond to Granny's remarks when he noticed my gaze, and understood my thoughts. For a moment he lowered his eyes, and then blushed intensely. I could hear his reply, his earnest and somehow timid voice: "There seem to have been no victims," and he bent his head. I was sorry to have hurt him with my childish curiosity. Who knows how he lost them, and the memory afflicted him. Perhaps he too had been very ill.

"I didn't think to heat up a drop of coffee for you," my grandmother said, rising to her feet.

"But please don't bother. If not, you know, I won't be able to sleep."

After a while he stood up, placing a hand on my hair, though averting his eyes in some other direction, and then he returned to his room, leaving the geranium on my night-table.

From that time onwards, Mr. Lin came back every evening. He would sit by my bed, and he talked with Granny. He never turned his eyes toward me, as though he were ashamed of something, whereas I looked constantly at him. His presence healed and transformed me. I was happy whenever I saw him, and hearing his soft voice was like listening to the music of the leaves in a sunlit garden. I would have wanted him to be there always. I felt that never again, in the whole of my life, would I ever see spiders if Mr. Lin remained at my side, and that I'd even be able to walk on the dark, nighttime sea if his hand were holding mine. Sometimes he noticed how I looked at him, and he'd ask, somewhat disturbed:

"Is anything wrong?"

And since I never replied, he'd place a hand on my head, with a fleeting smile, which enchanted me. Continuing to chat with Granny, he'd let his hand rest on my hair. "Certainly, Miss Brigida, pruning is advisable. But I think I'd wait a bit longer.... I've noticed that the *Maréchal Niel* has begun to bud.... Congratulations...."

"Mr. Lin, please don't go away...not ever...," I'd quietly remark.

"Don't think such things. Be a good girl."

His hand would lay sweetly on my forehead, and I'd calm down.

One morning—winter by now was finished, and spring was beginning with its transparent skies, with its hot winds, and the garden was full of colors—I awoke to a painful sensation: as if something very light, very dear, and close to my heart had fled, and had left me.

Granny appeared, bringing coffee and milk, and opened the window; and only then did I realize that her eyes were red behind her glasses, and her face quite drawn.

"You know.... Mr. Lin has had to leave," she said with hesitation. "He didn't want to wake you."

I cried in desperation.

"During the night," she said, when her voice came back, though trembling, "his wings suddenly sprouted. Already yesterday evening there were a few downy feathers.... I didn't want to mention it, so as not to upset you. You know," she continued, with a kind of thoughtlessness, "flowers and feathers, this season, sprout everywhere, and he had been waiting so long for them...."

"Mr. Lin! Mr. Lin!" I sobbed, "He won't come back... he'll no longer sit with us here in the evenings...."

"But he will come back. He promised," my grandmother said, holding back tears as best she could. "Many many years from now, if only you'll be good...you'll see him reappear, just as calm and cordial as that very first evening...."

"Do you believe that, Granny? Do you truly believe that?"

My tears subsided.

But the years have passed, Granny is gone. The garden too has disappeared, as well as that fine, intact and luminous sky which shined that day on my forehead. And Mr. Lin has never returned.

On what island has he settled? At the edge of what forest? Where is it now that he spends calm days, looking after flowers? And has he wholly forgotten our geraniums?

Sometimes, in the evening, when I'm at home alone, I seem to hear footsteps, and I imagine catching his affectionate voice: "But of course I can. Let me first just slip on my jacket." Though by now I'm a grown-up person, and have learned to use my reason, my heart starts to beat in the silence, darkly, and fills with a hope so fine and so painful that to see it come true might well be the end of me.

I halt for a while, looking up towards the door. Then I understand it was the wind.

Moonlight on the Wall

Olga Zachin, the blonde and beautiful wife of Carlo Zachin, the engineer, was expecting her second child, and pregnancy, this time around, had made her remarkably happy. But rather than pregnancy by itself, perhaps it was the season. She had had an argument with her husband, and then they had made up, and he had allowed her to visit her mother at the seaside for two weeks. The sea was very beautiful and smooth, the evenings were endless, and in the air was something tender, soft, and inexplicable, as though life had removed a mask and now showed its true face, its authentic treasures. Olga, stretched out on a deck chair with a book on her knees, couldn't manage to concentrate her thoughts on anything except herself and the mysterious beauty of being alive. It seemed to her, for the first time in her life, that a voice was whispering into her ear: "You don't know yourself, Olga, but you're intelligent, you're good, you have an extraordinary personality, and that's what makes you able to appreciate the beauty of life. Maybe," the voice insinuated, "you could keep a tighter rein on your sense of pride and make yourself a bit more accommodating."

This was true. The engineer's wife, in spite of her natural amiability, and a good education, was sometimes inclined to close up, to isolate herself, convinced that very few people (her husband, moreover, was not among them) appreciated her as much she deserved. She also resorted to rejoinders that might be a bit harsh. She wasn't to do that anymore. It brought her no gain. From now on she wanted to attempt to be a bit more humble, and more sensitive to other people's feelings. She wanted to be loved. By everybody. Nothing in the world could be more fascinating.

Upon returning to the city she found she had more available time than expected for nourishing such exemplary thoughts and feelings. Her husband had to be away for a few days. At home, for Massimo, their little son, there was a wonderful nurse. Every afternoon Olga went out for a walk.

She took long, slow strolls, very slow (she had to consider her condition), enchantedly savoring the life of the city. The light of the setting sun softened the shapes of the houses, lifted up the bridges, mysteriously widened the streets while the steps of the people walking through them sounded strangely light, and a kind of music enveloped everything. Friends of her husband passed by (the Zachins were quite well known) and raised their hats; there were girls with boyfriends who smiled in her direction from beneath their dark eyelashes; and in strollers there were babies who lifted their placid faces to gaze at her. The bells in the towers of the churches sounded uninterruptedly and Olga discovered herself in possession of grave and tender thoughts she had never thought before: "Everything is being born, the world is a scene of constant, radiant birth..." and "all of us have to be friends, we have to be friendly with one another." She was sorry to have passed so many years without having understood that. Nothing, surely, could have been more clearly true.

Almost every evening, at the end of her walks, Olga Zachin took a seat in a small café that she had frequently visited with her husband before they had married. And now, nostalgically, she found it again quite charming. It was at the end of a grand avenue, where the city became less luminous and less rich, and it seemed to possess a special silence that aroused her curiosity, a painful grace she had not discerned before. Along with a couple of run-down waiters, there worked in the place a little old woman to whom Olga immediately had taken a liking. She had the air of a person who has been waiting for something, or someone, for a good many years, or of a person who has a question to ask—she has it right there on the tip of her tongue—but who always forgets it. All in all, a poor little creature who had never been pretty, not even when young, in fact quite unpleasant to look at, with a mannish face, short legs, course white hair combed smooth and straight back, above a squarish forehead. Yet her dainty figure contrasted with the bold and slightly unhappy air of a person who had passed the whole of her life in menial labors, and who now was in semi-retirement. Perhaps she was a widow, a poor relative of the man who owned the place. She looked at Olga Zachin and smiled.

One evening, as children will do, almost furtively, she nodded to Olga as though having something she wanted to say to her. Olga was quite surprised, since usually, if she herself didn't make some initial show of cordiality, no one approached her, and on this particular evening she had been quite forgetful of the world. A fine moon hung above the wall that abutted the corner of the café, and Olga's thoughts were passionately turned to her husband. She'd have given who knows what to have him next to her. But she didn't grow rigid or show any sign of disdain, and indeed she smiled a little, disclosing that she had understood. And while preparing to leave, collecting her bag and her gloves, she approached the woman.

"I've been thinking," the woman said, "you'll have to

excuse me, please, because of course you don't know me—
but I've been thinking to ask if maybe tomorrow you'd like
to go to the movies with me. My treat. I never go to the
movies, I don't like to go alone. And now there's a really
good film...excuse me."

She had a rapid, peremptory voice, a man's voice, and,
at least at the moment, a little raucous. Olga didn't hurry to
give a reply.

"A really good film? What film?" she then demurely
asked. In the meanwhile she was thinking: "And this woman
is talking to the wife of Engineer Zachin! If she only knew!
Maybe it's my dress.... Not that it bothers me.... I didn't
realize, but maybe I'm badly dressed."

"*Brief Encounter*," the woman said.

There were two things that irritated Olga: that the film
the woman wanted to see was renowned for its sophistica-
tion ("Where," she uneasily wondered, "will she have heard
about it?"); and that she, Mrs. Zachin, should find that fact
to be irritating. The moonlight brightness seemed to have
diminished. She replied, vaguely:

"I have already seen it."

The aged waitress made no objection. It was just the
same as with men, "yes" and "no" when they don't find you
interesting, and equally when they do. Now the woman was
looking at her waistline.

"You're expecting," she said.

"Yes...." Olga replied. And then she considered adding, "That's why I don't much like to stay in closed spaces,"
but it struck her as pointless. The woman didn't seem
disappointed, nor to take her refusal as a reason for liking
her any the less. Her gaze rose from Olga's waistline to her
face, and that gaze overflowed with satisfaction.

"I have one too," she said after a while. Her hard chin
rose, her face trembled and settled, an ineffable joy wid-

ened her greyish eyes. "Sixteen years old. By now a man. Big and tall." She seemed with her words to have nodded a bow.

At that moment, the proprietor called her. She walked unhurriedly away on her short legs as though wearing a crown.

On the following evening, Olga Zachin returned there again. She had donned a more elegant dress, in light, white wool, decorated with heavy embroideries, white again, at the neck and wrists; on her head, a scarf in blue tulle, and shoes and bag again blue. She assured herself that the sharp and perhaps too forward manners of the old waitress hadn't offended her, but actually she felt a secret desire to see how far the familiarity, if not quite the temerity, of that stranger might go. She secretly wondered if her own beauty, and more than her beauty her graciousness, the impeccable style of every detail of her person and dress, were truly and wholly invisible to the woman in the café, "a closed book," as Carlo Zachin liked to say. Did they really make no impression on her? Olga had been ever so slightly humiliated. So she took a seat at her table and waited, but the woman, busy with cleaning the windows, gave no sign of seeing her and never abandoned her station.

"She's smug...she must be offended," thought Olga Zachin.

That night she couldn't manage to fall asleep. The child was a burden for her, and Carlo had sent her a card that put off his return for another week. She felt vexed and unhappy. The following morning, luckily enough, announced a wonderful day with a hot sun, clear skies, and all the presence, all the tremulous pleasure of springtime in the air. Olga went through the morning as though in a dream; instead of weighing her down, the child filled her with a kind of intoxication and she thought of Carlo intensely: she wanted to ask his forgiveness, when he returned, for her nervousness, for the way she was sometimes moody like a spoiled little girl. She wanted to be a real woman; full of understanding and capable of gentleness…and of still something more: of tenderness for the whole of life.

In the afternoon, after a light chicken lunch followed by some wonderful strawberries which Carlo had had delivered along with a charming note, she slept again and then woke up feeling far more rested and refreshed than usual. As though wafted along by this inexplicable happiness— she couldn't have moved, and surely didn't want to, so much as a finger against it—almost, indeed, as though she herself were an infant in a woman's womb and naturally destined to accept herself, she prepared to go out as usual…. She put on a dress more supple than the white one, a chiffon with yellow flowers and seemingly made of air, and matched it with a little necklace and bracelet of no particular value but very bright, in clear amber. She also put a bit of money in her purse since she wanted to give the woman a present. She vaguely felt that with that poor creature she hadn't quite adhered to the line she had chosen during her days at the sea, and she wanted tonight to be radiant.

First she went to the public park; then later she entered a small cool church at the back of a square. She prayed mechanically, but above all she thought about the world, about its beauty, about herself, about springtime and happiness. And she found herself thinking, almost tearfully, "I have still given nothing to life!" Her eyes were misty and yet full of a tender gaiety.

Exiting unhurriedly, she proceeded to the Corso and set to observing the windows of the stores. She had thought at first to buy flowers; but that was hardly the proper thing for a person of modest means and of such an age. Flowers would have been too much, or in any case out of place. The same for sweets, which, moreover, weren't lacking in that café. So she thought about something practical: a table cloth, or a couple of cups. But something practical was likewise inappropriate. They didn't know one another, and Olga might have given the impression of presuming that something was missing in the woman's home. No, the most proper and delicate thing, the thing that would show the most respect for the woman's personality (recalling her interest in that film) would surely be a book. Olga in fact had just been reading a simple and exquisite little volume, by a Frenchman, in a good translation: *The Bower*—a continuous if slightly romantic allusion to the happiness one can find in the cultivation of family affections, the little duties of everyday. The poor, she thought, take more pleasure in things like that than the rich.

She was lucky. She found the book immediately, and quite nicely bound. She also purchased a folder of elegant writing paper and had it included in the package, tenderly responding to the second thought that perhaps the woman's husband worked in some other city, likewise as a waiter; and if she didn't have a husband, surely her son would already have a girl friend and might find the gift useful. She had the package wrapped up in red paper and tied with a silver ribbon.

But when Olga Zachin entered the café, the woman wasn't there. And she didn't show up later. Olga was impatient and disappointed. Finally she rose to her feet, but before she left she asked the waiter why the woman hadn't been seen.

"She had to stay home," he replied laconically.

For a couple of days Olga Zachin didn't return to the café. There were things to be taken care of with the seamstress who made her dresses, and a storm or two in those two days had brought springtime to an ending. Tiresome winter seemed to have returned. Carlo had written that he'd be coming back home on Saturday, much love and kisses and don't do anything risky, and so Olga, a little annoyed, remained at home, always in the living room, receiving a few of her friends. But she asked the maid, on the second such evening, since she was free, to go to the café and deliver the book, along with abundant greetings "on the part of Mrs. Zachin."

When the maid returned she said she had left the book at the cash register, since the woman had not yet returned to work and was still at home.

"But why?" Olga Zachin indifferently asked while, seated at table, she tied a napkin beneath Massimo's chin.

"Her son just died," said the maid quite simply. And then she started towards the telephone, which had begun to ring. "It's for you, the Zanettis. They're thinking about going to the movies."

Olga would have wanted to tell the domestic to say that she was out. She was just that upset. But the girl had spoken quite loudly, forgetting in her usual carelessness to cover the phone with her hand, so Olga had no choice but to take the call and listen. Meanwhile, she was thinking that something quite serious had happened in the course of that extraordinary spring, in the midst of this happy city, in a remote corner of all of it, like a spot of rust on a dress. She felt aghast and humiliated, as though it were all her fault. She told the Zanettis she had a headache, but really her mind was turning back to the waitress' impassioned plea: when she had asked her to go to the movies. Certainly, now, the woman had to be thinking of something else and no longer of Olga Zachin. Life had collapsed.

"Oh yes, fine...he's doing quite well," said her trembling voice as she glanced at little Massimo. "Of course...

some other time...fine...thanks."

She laid down the receiver and returned to her seat at the table. She would have said that the light of the lamp had dimmed.

*   *   *

Olga had her baby a few days later. It was a difficult birth, and her beauty, contrary to predictions, came out of it wilted, along with her health. It was a difficult period for Carlo Zachin as well. A building commission he had worked quite hard to obtain was no longer to be realized. He entered a circle of new acquaintances that absorbed a good deal of his time and Olga even got the impression that he had lost his head for one of his Padua cousins. Luckily, however, the bad weather cleared up, the baby left an unhappy period behind him, that period of bottle nursing, and little by little life returned to normal. In addition, there was also the summer, which the Zachins that year decided to spend in the city; this made the couple a little sad, but they turned it all to the best by going out for long walks, in the evenings after dinner, that took them back to the time of their engagement.

Olga Zachin, naturally enough, was no longer so enchanted by life as she had been when she had found herself alone in the city, and her thoughts about people were no longer surrounded by the very same feelings she had experienced then. Indeed, she found constant torment in the thought of just how ingenuously she had wanted to give that book to the woman at that café, and how grotesque that gesture had been on a day of bereavement. With a kind of start, she every now and then surprised herself in the act of thinking back to that woman in a way that might have been appropriate to a person she knew quite well and who brought back to mind a world of former splendor. Ah, why had that woman lost her son, why had precisely *she* been the victim of such a tragedy? If only things had stayed the same as on the day before, and they still had the chance to exchange a few words about the film, and she had been able to pay her a compliment on her very fine taste. She imagined that such a balm might have touched the whole of her life.

One evening, ever so suddenly, as they were sitting at a table in the square, Olga asked Carlo Zachin to take her out for a bit of air…as far as that odd café on the outskirts of town. Carlo wasn't in the least opposed to the notion of walking for a bit, even if those bridges and canals and the proximity of the railway tracks always dampened his spirits.

So step by step they reached the place, and, just as a few months before, moonlight shone on the wall. And behind the wall, which enclosed a garden, someone was singing. Olga sat in the shadows, at a table on the sidewalk, and from there she suddenly saw, so strikingly, the expression of expectancy that held that face, just as it had struck her before, but with a wholly different empathy. There was the same hardness, the same attentiveness, the same profound and stony anxiety, as though of someone awaiting a reply. And yes, that reply had come, and it was terrible. But meanwhile music plays, continues to play, moonlight floods the wall, and over there, beyond it, lies a realm of festivity.

"Where, *over there?*" Olga Zachin found herself thinking. "Where are we? And what is this wall?"

She looked at the woman with a gaze that was full of supplication, as though the woman were so much farther ahead of her and had learned the truth, as though the coarseness of her figure mysteriously gave off light. But the woman no longer saw her; she no longer had any awareness of Olga Zachin.

The Tree

Last Saturday as the first snow began to fall, just towards five in the afternoon, I found myself at the Central Station, having accompanied a person to a train. At first I didn't realize it was snowing, but it struck me on returning to the open air that something in the tone and color of the great, broad square had changed. It was the very same square that all of us can visit at any hour of the day or night, to the right the large hotel surmounted by a flattened dome, and on the left the tramway tracks, leading towards the center of town past a variety of cafés where brightly lit windows open back through a whitish haze to a glimpse of the reds and yellows of bottles of liqueurs. But the cafés, and I grasped this only after a moment or so, were all dark and empty, though open, and no trams were running, not so much as the most distant clanging of their bells. I thought there must have been a power failure in this part of the city, perhaps elsewhere too, and I made up my mind to go back to my hotel on foot. After all, it was not very far away, and the weather was not cold.

As I looked about, searching for the street to take (at least ten streets run out from this square), the indistinct sensation of just a few moments before returned to me, but now with the weight of a true disturbance: the sensation that something abnormal had taken place. This place in which I found myself was not Milan, no more than Hamlet and Ophelia had been citizens of England. The plain-looking houses that rise in the many streets around the square seemed evanescent and flushed with a heart-rending pallor. Their walls appeared to shine from some interior source and were no longer lit by starlight, or by any ray of brightness belonging to the world of our own. "It must always be like this, at certain hours of the year, and my seeing it now is easily explained by a particular fragility of my nerves."

I started down Via P___, and from there would cross Piazza Grande and reach my hotel. Skirting close to the walls, I once again felt strangely intent, like a person who only shortly before had received an important piece of news, a very personal piece of news. But, to tell the truth, I couldn't remember what it might have been. So my calm began little by little to creak and give way like a sheet of ice over a stream of warm, black water murmuring and fleeing beneath it.

"Let's see," I said to myself. "The hotel. Everything there okay. The bill paid up. Work to do for tomorrow... quite fine. Let's see what else." And then I suddenly grasped the reason for that sense of dismay I had felt at the station exit. My dismay resided in a banal yet quite alarming fact: I no longer had any idea of whom I had accompanied to the station.

"But nothing could be more normal," I remarked to myself after a moment's reflection. "When we're highly fatigued, even the name of what month it is, or of the season, can slip our minds. Maybe it wasn't even an important name. At any rate, I'll shortly recall it again."

I wanted to give myself a rational explanation for what had occurred, but no sooner had I put my finger on it than I ceased to be at peace. I might have said that a mouse had slipped inside my dress and found its way up close to my heart, where at first it nibbled gently and then with greater zeal, striking deeper. Finally it bit to the pulse and seat of life itself, and I reeled with a lacerating pain.

The mouse fled. I saw it run away directly from in front of me and then across the street to hide at the curb, from where it watched me with a strange flashing brightness in the tiny pupils of its eyes. But even though the pain was still horrid and the beast right there, I refused to own up to it. "The weather is really changing," I remarked to myself. "This twinge is a warning. I'll drink a small cup of hot rum as soon as I'm back in my room."

I began to feel cold, but paid it no attention as I trained my eyes upwards here and there onto those buildings that looked so dead while yet suffused with a vague spark of dawn, an uncertain reflection; those facades where not a single door or window stood unshuttered to allow the glimpse of a face, a light, where not a single voice resounded, not a sound, not even the faintest cadence of passing footsteps. "At this hour, in Milan, everyone is asleep," I continued to spin out to myself. "It's a city of workers. They go to bed early, by nine o'clock."

A clock from a distant church—a clock, seemingly, that wasn't quite sure of this world, and with a clapper that resounded with a clear grave music—struck five hours and two quarters.

"There's one of those clocks that gets stuck," I mumbled after a moment.

I reached the park, and here I realized that it was truly snowing, quite heavily. The snow fell from the sky like a whirlpool of light, and when looked at steadily it gave the impression of swirling back upwards. It rose and fell. How beautiful! It never touched the ground. Large, transparent flakes of snow just barely caressed the branches of certain trees and then melted away. It seemed a hand that wants to write out something portentous and immense, or to stroke a forehead, and which instead continually repents, trembles and vanishes. One felt a vague, deep desire to be ravished into that raiment of light, to hover upwards from the black earth and flee into a place made only of serenity, music, and joy. And why was that not to happen?

There was a bench and I approached it. I sat down, and remained there quietly to look around me as I held the upturned collar of my coat tightly against my face. In the spinnings and reversals of that eddying of white, inside that magnificent calm, as though a mantle of candid velvet were rushing to fold itself around the world, I heard a remote and harmonious echo. The clock again, a song of hours. Memories unwound through my mind, but without fever. I saw my mother and father in the sunlit garden, I listened to the ceaseless sound of the March wind on the hill. Then, at a certain point, all these images and sounds of light disappeared, and I saw myself again in this city. I saw myself in my hotel room as I prepared to go out and turned off all the lights.... Yes, *all the lights suddenly went out*, and my mind lapsed back into its great confusion, and again the sensation of a brutal pain at my heart. Surely something had happened. There was no longer room for doubt.

I would have given anything at all to have been left unreminded of it, and to let everything remain exactly as it was, with neither form nor name. I got up from the bench, and, vacillating, fixing my eyes as best I could in front of me, set out to where I thought I would find the exit.

But the exit was no longer there, or at least it lay hidden beneath the fallen snow. However, there was a great number of trees. Their black, twisted roots almost drew up from out of the ground, and some of them seemed to be human beings—men deprived of everything and close to the end of their lives—who huddled now against a wall and cried. In pure and absolute silence, the snow continued to fall on these creatures. I walked in their midst, and would have said they silently stepped aside to allow me through. Never before, here in the park, had I realized the presence of so many trees, and all so sensitive. The sight of them began to feel oppressive, and to frighten me. Why were they suffering? I felt quite fine, entirely fine. No, it wasn't on my account.

"The hotel should be somewhere close by," I began again to repeat to myself with absurd intensity. "The windows will all of course be dark, but the entrance will be bright and full of people. There's Corrado, Daniele, the lovely Iris, the others."

A sign, quite large and just like the ones that parade along the highways, hung at the top of a pole fixed into the earth. Gigantic letters, in sharp, bright green, spelled out these words before my eyes:

SILENCE. DISAPPEARED. TRANQUILITY.

"Disappeared" was the word I stared at most, entranced. It awakened my heart to such a depth of echoes and suspicions as to arouse a veritable terror that sucked all the heat from my forehead, and for an instant I was embraced by immobility itself.

"So even now," I continued, while drawing a sigh that released me from this horror, "they insist on putting up signs on the grass, as though that hadn't been proved already to be so entirely useless...." As I said this, my eyes, which brimmed with tears for absolutely no reason, ranged off to a large open space where a small monument to Cavour once stood. The small monument was no longer there, and in its place was a dazzling tree, rising to a great height.

This time I said nothing; but as I shook myself, pushing away the anxiety that dashed like a crazed bird against the walls of my skull, I looked at this solitary, towering tree of ice which stood before me and I attempted to see it as nothing more than the puerile artifice of a Christmas tree. But those branches were decorated with nothing but ice, even the trunk was encased in ice, and the peak blazed only with a light of ice. Here and there from out of the whiteness hung sharp, pointed, gleaming daggers of the muted blue that only ice assumes.

A supreme need to ignore the meaning of what was happening drew me to the base of that tree, to gaze upward, just like any other citizen, in admiration of its wintry metamorphosis; and that was where I stood, smiling though cold and full of pain, when the tree first moved: laden and sparkling with its burden of frost, it bent down and touched my forehead. I retreated, and the creature moved again.

Its roots had withdrawn from the earth, like paws, and they weakly advanced through the light-filled snow. They advanced to follow me. This, naturally enough, was a dream, though a horrid dream. So while hurrying my steps as best I could toward where I imagined the gates of the park to be, I set to repeating my eternal, monotonous, refrains: "Work, okay; tomorrow, Sunday…; phone Corrado…; let's see what else." As I ran these statements through my weakened, submerging mind, the apparition of ice and branches slithered up beside me on its pitiful roots and emitted a sound I'm sure you could hardly have heard without crying. It was just that various, and profound, and similar to a human life.

"Those branches really do creak," I remarked from out of my obstinate desire to lie to myself, "but I would never have imagined that snow could so much resemble metal. And, yes, of course it's that this tree has grown so light that the wind can waft it along like a leaf while making its boughs resound with such an enchanted noise...."

While thinking these phrases I began to run towards the gates, which stood there, I could see them, facing into Via Boschetti. I came out into the street and halted, though still with the sense that this supernatural creature of ice was just behind my shoulder, because my heart was about to explode.

At this point, finally safe, I faintly desired to see and hear the tree once again, as though that conjunction of light and pain had held the hidden secret, the name, the thing, everything the nature of which I could not understand, that had made my heart that night go mad.

But I did not see the tree again. Instead, here I was at Porta Venezia, then Viale Vittorio Veneto and the high embankment at the edge of the park, and my hotel.

This large, modern building, eighteen storeys tall, its walls wounded by over a thousand windows, stood before me, and I stopped. I exclaimed, "At last!" but with a voice that was broken by regret and by a longing for a truth from which I had subtracted myself, fearing to look it in the face; and simultaneously I was struck by something extraordinary.

To the front of the hotel atrium, where a little elevator ordinarily runs and where friends are always coming and going, to the front of this atrium now brightly lit but totally empty, two goldfinches of precisely the size of a human form were roosted on a branch covered with snow, a branch which issued from the wall above the glass door, almost as though the wall itself were earth and the hotel a forgotten garden.

Their small, round eyes, round and black, were fixed,

bright, and melancholic; and a song both acute and I could not say if more sweet or full of desperation—a song which spoke of tenderness and farewell, of the hope of regaining the woods, and the doubt, and of a joy besieged by cold and nothingness—issued from their motionless beaks. These birds were dead. With their fiery foreheads and black and yellow wings, and perched on delicate legs of a material that seemed to be gold, they were dead and already cold beneath their silken plumage. Their song, a memory. Faced with their death and their gracefulness, I suddenly understood why the city was dark, why the mouse had gnawed at my heart, why the tree laden with ice had pulled itself up from out of the ground to come and offer me company, singing songs about the past. I understood *who* I had accompanied to the station and *who* those two marvelous shadows of birds had to be. I understood as well that my youth, which I had attempted to forget with all my repeated phrases, "fine...let's see...the bills...fine...tomorrow...," I understood that my youth, and everything else which you too will have lost, had everywhere, that night, returned; frightened and full of sobs, it had run like a girl along this pitiful earth.

The House
in the Woods

The house where I presently live is at the top of a slightly rising, moderately tree-lined road, flanked on either side by rows of buildings identical to my own, outwardly dull and apparently empty. At the summit of the hill lies a smallish square (if this term can apply to a space that has no shops and no massive doors that open back to court-yards) and here, to the left of a gate and garden concealing the house, is a narrow path. This lane grades downward, and quick as a girl some five or six years old (it is just that short) it fairly plummets along the edge of the wood that faces the garden, and twenty yards later it broadens and vanishes in front of a vast park of extraordinary beauty. This park, from what I have been told, is the property of a charitable institution, the activities of which unfold in a neoclassical villa that whitens—in winter, when the vegetation thins—among trees and box-wood hedges.

The eye is unable to discover the limits of this park, which is known by the antique name of the *Rinascenza*. Toward the north it recedes into incredible distances, descending first into a valley and then rising, it seems, towards bluish heights and a tenuous wave-like ridge of mountains.

To return to the house that interests me, or rather to

the area where the house was built, the area between the house and the Rinascenza, meaning just beyond the woods, and all around the premises of this oh so charitable institution: this area is dotted with a snowfall of little white and pinkish homes, lost among still further stands of trees and more modest stretches of lawn. For anyone surveying the whole of the scene from the top of the path or from one of the upper floors (to which I once climbed) of the building where I live, the general impression is of such intense and almost supernatural beauty as to leave one mute. The silence is clouded, so to speak, only by the whispering wings of the pink and yellow butterflies that flutter through the air for three quarters of the year. No voice sounds (unless by night an owl, or at dawn a blackbird) and you might just as well be gazing down at Eden.

All this, barely a step away from a teeming City which still today, I am told, is fairly congested and a true hotbed of Ideas! Here, no ideas, nor even Motors: only calm, voluptuousness, and sleep.

Let's return to the house where I live.

It is five storeys tall, each storey decked with lovely terraces (where no one is ever to be seen) and with two apartments to a floor, which gives at least twenty tenants (reckoning two people to each apartment). I am personally acquainted (and I have lived here for about ten years) with no more than two or three of them: an elderly gentleman, a stout lady, and a girl, perhaps a student, who is fairly pleasant. But no one ever has a word for anyone other than his or her dog; and none of them, even more notably, ever betrays the slightest gaze of appreciation for all the beauties I have just described. And all of them together emit not the slightest rustle of clothing or the scrape of a shoe as they move about. So I have acquired the habit of thinking of *like Celati's puppet figures*

them as *painted* figures, or as figures just outside the bounds of my imagination. And there are no other people, or I have not seen them, in the whole of this succulent region.

But now to my own apartment. It's on the building's ground floor, and even though it's reachable, quite ordinarily, by way of a door that opens into the vestibule—shielded in turn by a great glass door in the middle of the courtyard garden—it can *also* be entered from a terrace that stretches for about ten yards beneath the windows of the so-called *living room*. This terrace then angles to the left and continues its course in front of two french-windowed balconies on the right-hand side of the living room. So the living room, finally, has all of six openings, counting ordinary windows, balconies, and a vast picture window; and the curious thing—despite *so many* openings (none of which, moreover, is obscured by blinds, shutters, or drapes)—is that the light which enters the room is eternally the light of dusk.

In one part of the living room (the southern zone) there's a folding curtain of heavy plastic; and behind this curtain (this started about ten years ago) a relative lives here with me. But for the moment I'll say nothing more about that.

On the left-hand side of the living room—or the Chamber of Night, as it might more fittingly be called—is a sort of corridor (stretching to the rear of the house) which I'd like to refer to as the Hallway of Fears. I have attempted vainly to hang it with patterned red crepe drapes on which playing cards vie with cheerful bottles of wine. But it remains a silent corner from which anything, absolutely *anything*, can find its way in. This hallway was probably conceived by the Architect—whom I have never met, but surely a neurotic Architect—for the sole and singular purpose of creating a mood of expectation: an air of empty, cruel suspension (rooted in an unhappy childhood, resulting in a penchant for vengeance) but balanced, I must add, by a fairly successful attempt to call up a sense of relief, a sense, I'd say, of repose. At least that's the feeling one gets from the microscopic fireplace in the south-west corner of the living room (remembering that the hallway is on the north-east, whereas the façade looks entirely toward the west, where the woods are.)

In the whole of a fairly bleak house, this hearth is the center of all the refreshment that a mind too absorbed in silence and whatever may have woven its warp and woof can hope to enjoy.

Yes, I truly adore this fireplace.

It stands at the base of a wall about seven feet tall and painted an old rose hue, unlike all the other walls which are a spent green—spent and (I'll add) *very* dirty. I have hung up over the mantle-piece two or three framed reproductions of the works of a French artist of the eighteenth century, a few rag-dolls, and some handcrafted objects from Germany (clocks and chimes), and it's here, when life's assorted business is not going well or when the wind bites the summit of the trees in the wood, that I come to think.

I love it most of all in October, but surely I am never averse to sitting beside it in the spring as well, or on deep winter nights; next to it there's a low easy chair upholstered in a dry, pink velvet and dubbed *Grand-Mère*, flanked by chests of drawers and bedsteads in brightly painted wood, which constitute the furniture of the Chamber of Night.

Now, very succinctly, a phrase or two about the rest of the house, and then I'll proceed to the OCCURRENCE (fairly indefinable) that makes for the subject of this story.

It's composed, the rest of the house, of I don't know how many little rooms, corridors, and closets, all of them *uninhabitable* (another of the Architect's ideas, or a multiplication of his fears) until finally at the back on the NORTH-EAST side, directly facing the Rinascenza (which, however, remains concealed by the high courtyard wall) one finds two tiny passages: the place true and proper where I live. The first of these passages would be totally dark if it weren't for a glass door that opens into the other, where I study; so the first takes a part of the cold eastern light from the second, and from its window on the courtyard.

Next to these two rooms, or cubbyholes, one enters, by way of a narrow hallway, into a frightfully cold and decrepit Kitchen, and from there, by way of a rickety flight of stairs, one descends into the courtyard, which the Architect, once again, decided to place *at the back* of the house.

I can't begin the story true and proper without a brief description of this Courtyard.

It runs along the whole of the back of the house, extending beyond it, on the south, by five and a half meters, forming the ideal space for a second house, which I have always—strangely enough—seen rising there, an invisible and much more rational house, and therefore a much more pleasant house, than the real house where I live!

But we can leave such fantasies alone.

Since the courtyard runs the length of the house, plus, as already mentioned, another five and half meters, and since the back of the house measures fifteen meters and thirty centimeters long, the total length of the courtyard therefore amounts to twenty meters and eighty centimeters: precisely the height, if one could lay it down flat, of a five storey building!

Its width, on the other hand, is 7.9 meters. So almost eight.

The height of the wall that girdles the courtyard on three of its other sides measures two meters and forty centimeters. A height, for my modest stature, that it is practically unreachable.

But the north wall, on the left—for anyone descending the stairs from the kitchen—is a great deal higher, say four meters tall in the area near the stairs, and then three at the center, until reaching the height of the rest of the wall, two meters and forty centimeters, at the northeast corner.

The *primary* elements of the Secretness of the Courtyard:

First of all, the *wall:* not because of its height, but owing to the faded mousey color of its paint, it grips you by the heart. The grey of the paving tiles, counting two thousand and nine hundred (having counted them myself!) The grey of the clouds that come from over the Rinascenza (hidden by the wall) and pass above the courtyard, often bringing me a damp smell of rain, and thus a peace that I do not possess.

In conclusion, another element of the terrible Secretness of the Courtyard is a series of little windows that open at ground level; I have always believed, and perhaps it is true, that they illuminate a garage. Especially there's the "bricked-up" window, placed *beneath* the stairs, which seems, instead, to open back onto a sewer that drains the entire building.

Ah, how many times have I walked in this courtyard on autumn and winter nights, evenings, and afternoons! Here on this hill the air is very fine, thanks to the endless vista of woods that surround it; and thanks to the moisture of the clouds and the wind, which blows in general throughout the whole blessed year.

I could call myself happy if only there were some small grate in this wall, interrupting not so much its uniformity as its Blindness.

The Architect, in denying this wall a grate or fence or any kind of happy opening out toward the Rinascenza and the other woods, must have had some purpose of his own, some highly moral purpose, and I acquiesce to it. But I do not want to conceal, here, that I have always darkly desired a window in that wall, a fissure through which to catch a glimpse of the green magnificence of the Rinascenza's park. But, more than impossible, a thing like that is essentially unthinkable; and the proof of that drastic prohibition (in regions of the soul where everything impossible in fact takes place) is that never, not even once in the course of my daily life throughout these past ten years, have I attempted to carry a chair, or two chairs, or some kind of stepladder into the courtyard, so as to lift my chin to the top of the wall. That would be an easy thing to do, but I have never done it. And perhaps less for moral reasons than for something deeper. I am convinced that higher decisions preside over the lives of human beings, and if I find myself in this house, in this courtyard, and if this courtyard is deep, impervious and blind, well, there must be a reason. I do not want to search it out.

I return to the Kitchen in Decrepitude and will tarry a moment before returning to the Chamber of Night, since here there's a detail that stands at the start of my melancholy trials (which stand at the start of the story). A banal detail, if you like, but highly important: the ruin of the sink, or rather of its several pipes—a ruin that results in a constant water loss, so that the bills, owing to excessive consumption, modest as they are, are approaching astonishing sums. On account of this sink, at the start, I mobilized all of my acquaintances in the Capital, some of them quite notable; and all the persons to whom I had turned replied with the promise, in due time, of sending me a plumber. But no such thing, alas, had ever worked out. All sorts of crucial occurrences have taken place in the history of the world, during these last ten years, and all of us have witnessed them, so there's no real need for me to recount them, what with the collapsing of governments and republics, and the demise of empires, and the founding of others; the appearance of new civilizations that hurl themselves (like shipwrecked sailors against wretched shoals) against old civilizations; and blood, and sermons in the churches and the public squares. There has even been talk, with a certain self-indulgence, of the Apocalypse, and the Horsemen of the Stratosphere have frequently troubled the nights of unfortunate souls whose eyes have peered out through the windowpanes of New York, or London, or Lisbon. But my plumber has never shown up.

So a huge bucket inhabits the space beneath the sink, ETERNALLY, and anyone who enters the kitchen, at night, will hear I couldn't say what kind of crying, a muffled groan, a timid, respectful knocking at some invisible door.

Toc toc toc!

And then TOC TOC TOC!

And then, in the deadest hours:

ic + tic + ic!

Signor Raggi

It was one of those March or end of February nights that follow in the wake of particularly turbid days: hot winds blown in from the coast of Africa encounter the eternal succession of Atlantic storms, and these—as they clash with the frigid air masses that the North continually disposes on the Alps and the Left-hand Sea, and that the Atlantic winds cannot cross—these form gales of driving aqueous fury that mix with the golden dusts of Africa. What we have is not the sirocco, but the *mausin*, a wind normally known by a host of other names, but always remaining the terrible, arid wind of desert Africa: blinding dust, and in great enormous swirls! Oily chocolate-colored clouds that muddy the earth. And in the midst of it, as though from myriad cracks in the walls, some touch of ice, of wetness, and of heat! And most of all a song! An inarticulate, savage song, sometimes similar to a wail, at others to a threat, at others to a long recital of victims, at others to souvenirs of childhood beatitudes, and adolescent graces! When it blows across the sea, it fills the waves (in my memory) with an apricot light, very pure and yet unhealthy! All the bells held trapped in that wind begin to sound, even the bells of foundered ships, even the bells of the funerals of the poor. You survey the whole of your life and would like to cry, but the sockets of your eyes hold nothing but two small stones. (And this, Reader, is how weather transfigures nature!)

So the wind, after just such a day, gave no sign now of letting up, and indeed continued to increase. I had never before heard the likes of such a *mausin*; and so much so that the ring of the telephone, which oddly was not out of order, didn't make me nervous at all, but, quite to the contrary, brought me I wouldn't know quite what kind of urgent comfort. Moreover, to remain in drab reality as wholly as possible, or at least to attempt to remain there, I was still—on a thread of both hope and desperation—awaiting the arrival of Signor Raggi (as luminous a name as the aura that surrounded his person, by now, after ten full years). This Signor Raggi was a benevolent plumber, worthy of all reverent thoughts, whom a powerful personage of the Capital (I cannot name the illustrious Place) had finally conde-scended to send to me. But he hadn't arrived. Our appoint-ment had been set for the Third Hour of the afternoon, but

he had not come! A telephone phone call from the office of
the illustrious Place had announced a delay: of no more
than two hours. Raggi was to visit me at five. So with my
heart in my throat I had waited until five o'clock, prey to the
anguish inflicted by the wind, to the silence of the neighboring room (where the *person* I have not named emitted no
sign of life or the slightest gesture of friendship—since this
is the state of mind most typically rendered acute in this
person by *mausin* weather), and finally to the odious thought
of what was happening beneath the sink. For the last two
days a pipe had been threatening to break, and in the
morning its condition had grown more grave. Blasted and
muddy, water now wound its way, like a greenish snake, all
the way to the door; only a heap of rags had stopped it
(temporarily). But I didn't dare to think about what was
taking place in the kitchen; my only hope was that the
pavement, which slants slightly towards the stairs, would
convey the water towards an outlet, or its natural estuary:
meaning the Courtyard.

But if a cunning reader, chary of faith in realities
purported to lie behind narrative, and ready indeed to look
askance at the naive ploys that narrators are likely to field
to attract attention—in these times so indisposed to all
attention—if any such readers were now to imagine that
this Raggi will shortly be revealed as the basic element of
my story, and an element charged with humor, they will
soon come away disappointed and confused. I was waiting
quite factually for Signor Raggi, and the Kitchen's conditions were precisely as I have just described them; but that
was surely not the grounds for my anxiety, or for the melancholy terror that sat by now beside me, in the Chamber
of Night.

Since by now it was dusk, indeed the very heart of a

lengthening evening (on the verge of turning into Night), my ears seemed to catch a sound of fatigue in the *mausin*, or at least of uncertainty, unless, in ways unperceived by myself and the surrounding woods, it was preparing, after an illusory lull, to provoke even greater harm. I have no idea of what was wrong with me. I felt I wanted to cry, though without having, as I then remarked, so much as an available teardrop. Fear and irritation had so embraced my soul that no free corner was free for even a modest sigh. At eight, and then at nine, and then at ten o'clock, Raggi had not appeared, and so I ceased to expect him. The copse beyond the windowpanes, lit by a sliver of a moon, which had opened a chink for itself in the midst of so much storm, seemed in every way like a great green Thorax, with its vault of bones and its sacred organs, which were only clots of wind that huddled among the branches (though all around was peace) and continually moaned: uh uh!

I had already inspected the courtyard—balancing quite carefully on the windowsill of my room—and I had looked with the aid of a flashlight into all of its nooks. I had checked that the ground-level windows were properly padlocked and that the opening into the sewer was still bricked up. I had watched the clouds as they scudded eastward, their ballrooms billowing with light and then obscured by lunar curtains, and I presumed the *mausin* to have found its route. But all the same, I didn't feel at ease. So, while returning through the length of those darkened hallways to the room overlooking the woods, I had bolted the doors one after the other behind me; to close myself in completely, I then barred the passage to the corridor (the Hallway of Fears) with a heavy chest of drawers. But this chest, unfortunately, did not completely block the wind, which continued to gust through the house, sometimes thrusting an impertinent hand against the back of the cretonne curtains and showing me *five spread fingers*, the meaning of which I could not understand. I prudently averted my eyes.

This, in short, was the situation at eleven o'clock in the evening: *mausin* in departure behind the moon, and cold air flooding from the west; broken clouds above the woods; water menacing from the kitchen; silence, and this enormous picture window for a snob-class house. I was certain that all the World's Masked Faces would soon burst through it.

Clearly a baleful situation.

One allowing for no other remedy, my crafty Reader, than to light a crackling fire.

Which is what I was rapidly to do.

The Fireplace

Fire is said to hold at bay the Beasts that threaten the life of the wayward hunter. There are times when a wax match and a fistful of dried brush can mean salvation. One forgets to add, however, that fire discourages insects, inclusive of flies and giant mosquitoes, and repels as well (above all) the Arachnids that dwell in forests, and which in general infest the houses near woods.

Since I am terribly afraid of Arachnids, I have always made certain, ever since coming to live in this house, that the fireplace is ready at any hour of the night to send up its smoke and to frighten away, with a gust or two of blinding heat if not with smoke alone, whatever mysterious creatures might by chance have sought shelter beneath the furniture—creatures which from there might attempt a sortie towards the *Grand-Mère*. An ample and very warm blanket (such creatures have a horror of wool) augments the defense, and a dim light, which burns beneath the tiny MASK of an English Fool squatting on the mantlepiece rounds out my security measures. William—as the Mask is named— is so horrid and grim that the insects—simply on seeing him—are instantly dismayed, whereas the grace of his smile (ah, how human, how great a herald of crystaline waters and civil company) would disarm the most threatening of Specters!

That, in short, was the situation: defense and melancholy.

Melancholy

Yes, melancholy; why not call it by its name? All of our lives contain moments when it seems—when the feelings, in fact, quite clearly declare—that we are *desperately* removed from our *natural* place; moments of knowing that life (or something higher than life) quite clearly intended to undo us, simply by inventing us, an act itself which indulged a will to punish. You feel a fluttering desperation, an unbearable racing of the heart. You search for the door (to get out of this place) knowing from the start that it cannot be found. There is no door, no exit, from this situation: the courtyard wall is insurmountable, the doors lead nowhere. Outside is Eden, paradise, the seven beatitudes and the nine wonders of the world; all the world's meadows, woods, and pink and yellow butterflies; and the clouds and the sea and the common people who offer such comfort to ailing hearts; and the normal, so thoroughly consoling occupations. Yet there is nothing for you. Only your studies, your table, the lamp you turn off at noon, the solitary sun from the depths of the grounds of the Rinascenza, nothing more. But no, I am wandering astray: I also have the evenings, the measured and thoughtful nights at the side of the fire, looking at the fire, there beneath that little statue of William, and thinking of long past times when there were happy feasts, and perhaps when Mr. William (as cousin, husband, or grandad makes no difference) was a member of the closest family!

One thinks about other things, about the riddles of time and space (beyond the clouds, beyond the *mausin*, beyond the world's fair seasons). About where it all comes from (and may be going). Then, finally, or little by little, one no longer thinks at all.

There's an old nursery rhyme:

> The kitten, beside the fire,
> falls little by little asleep.

And thus, though no longer a cat, or tiger, or kitten of cat or tiger, and having been that way by now for a good number of years, the author of these lines—the *Prolegomena* in one of her hands and the *Bible* in the other—fell asleep.

The "Plumbers"

Two men of indeterminate age, both dressed in workmen's overalls, were walking about in the Chamber of Night when, owing to a gust of unpleasantly icy air, I suddenly awakened. They must surely have been wearing felt moccasins, since their shoes didn't sound so much as the slightest creak. But they weren't wearing gloves, and so I can't understand why the various joints of their brownish fingers made no noise among the objects they in fact were *moving*. These objects amounted, at least for the moment, to a few old curtains that lay in a heap on the floor, off to one side of the picture window; so these men must have taken them down from their rods. There were also a couple of cushions, a broken lamp, and some other miserable odds and ends.

Since all of these things ("historically speaking" is what I'd like to say, as a suitably solemn phrase, but that might be going too far) were *entirely and completely* worthless from a monetary point of view, the only deduction I could possibly draw from this operation was that the house had flooded while I was asleep and that these *poor plumbers*, sent by Signor Raggi, were trying to stem the water that by now was everywhere. So I looked all around and made an uncertain inspection (between sleep and wakefulness) of the whole of the floor. It was utterly *dry*. The only thing wrong was the frigid wind that continued to invade the room. But then I could see it was coming from the casement at the side of the room's great picture window: its tall thin pane of glass had been removed and propped upright against the radiator.

A clock, standing next to William and sparkling with imitation gold, showed four o'clock in the morning.

So now, already, we had reached the first day of March!

The fire in the fireplace seemed still to be lit—but only embers and the stump of a log.

I felt an indefinable twinge of annoyance, and, behind it, of apprehension. I found it so odd that these two plumbers hadn't rung the bell, and had set to work (but what work?) without ever having spoken a word to me.

A thought came into my mind: they are thieves. But that thought, in a certain sense, left me indifferent.

I'll pretend they are really plumbers, I said to myself in that somehow natural (or infantile) haze of dementia typical of a sleep that doesn't wish to be disturbed. And therefore, fearing with ever greater horror that the cold would wake me up entirely, I *addressed* them in a muddled and plaintive voice—of which my consciousness was aware and for which it reproved me—begging them "to be kind enough, please, to close *at least* that window." The cold was waking me up.

But there was no reply, except for a muffled grumbling: the kind of sound that's sometimes made, as they lift suspicious foreheads, by underpaid workers, or by gentlemen pained by the circumstance of having been mistaken for workers.

"The window," I repeated, "PLEASE."

The young man on the right, who was dark and seemed reserved, or had even an air of suffering—and whom I'll call Antonio—shot the quickest of glances toward his companion. A meaningful but not malevolent glance. This companion was quite a different sort of person: he was tall, and excellent teeth flashed at the bottom of the white mask which covered his face…making me think (I was and remain just that far removed from reality) that these men were surely actors, and that the second would have to be *Pulicino*, that figure from even earlier than Roman times and of whom one finds a mention in some of the Sannite chronicles.

"Am I disturbing you?" I at this point asked with a smile.

"Not at all," they replied, their voices quite civil and free of all resonance. (Ah, yes, my heart! Their voices were *soundless*.)

For a while, though perhaps for only a very few minutes, I simply sat and watched what they were doing. My sadness, Reader, was enormous. I brimmed with the utterly terrible awareness that those two figures were *neither plumbers, nor thieves, nor actors*, nor anything else that the world can name, not even that invisible matter that physics discusses in its moments of dream. An awareness so strong that the most resigned calm, which is the faithful companion of all such terrors, had taken charge of my soul. From that point on I made up my mind to remain where I was and to observe, hoping my own particular rôle in these evil and frightful events would be nothing more than that of a hapless spectator.

Now the cold in the room was truly rigid, heightened as it were by a tone of *animosity* on the part of the great plastic curtain at the shoulders of the *Grand-Mère* (and at my own). The curtain had sufficiently parted to reveal in the background a miserable little bed (miserable but not sad) where a "person" was seated in an attitude that was partly ironic and partly allusive, or perhaps partly resigned. And this "person," whom till now I have not named—in a certain sense not even remembering her existence (since I do not like her)—was *Grand-Mère* herself, the person who lends her name to the pink velvet easy chair, but who never comes into this room, nor into any of the others. She's a person, curious Reader, whom you too certainly have met in your life, as well as in your memories, since she is someone who doesn't belong specifically to me or specifically to you, but to all those people who are gifted with mind and memory: she is the bruised and swollen side of one's own soul.

Trude (or Trade)—since that is her name, her provisional name, you understand—corresponds to the part, quite actually swollen, of your soul or of the city or the sprawling village that you have left behind you, by growing up or by not growing up. That forgotten part, land, or home. And though she must be a thousand years old, or more, or less, her character has remained unchangeable: an aggressiveness—constant, you understand—and a tough, untiring avidity (later I'll tell you for what) that make her more trying and baleful than even the *mausin.* I had never believed she was truly there, hidden asleep behind the curtain, but now I was sure of it: there was no true fear on her hard, arid face, which struck me indeed as delighted to descry all the tiniest details of the events taking place. I also understood why I had been able until now to endure the foreboding of the secrets of the house: because the house was also inhabited by this honest, violent Person named Trude.

This was the moment when with one bright eye she winked in my direction, while the other surveyed a group of "figurines" (barely larger than a toy) that stood on the floor, on the threshold between the two rooms: a representation of three young Citizens—three young women in modern dress and in the act of counting money.

Those faces, Reader, showed total deprivation.

No rouge, no natural beauty, no feelings of any kind at all, neither hateful nor pleasant. Nothing, absolutely nothing, except for a few scant items of reality—such as bone, flesh, skin, and various bundles of nerves might be—gave any kind of substance to those graceless faces, of which the natural color was uncertain. But the hands of these three Woman Citizens—hands that were serious and conscientious and that shared that uncertain color—meanwhile recorded the serial numbers of enormous quantities of banknotes. Other monies—in the form of rings and earrings—sparkled at their side in a black plastic bag. And that is all. I do not know their names, and if I knew them I would not speak them. These girls, moreover, I perceived immediately, were nothing more than happenstance Extras in the story. They had no other rôle to play.

And now, the following dialog:

TRUDE (*to me, not naming me, as a slight*): You'll tell these gentlemen that I've had my suspicions about them for quite some time.

ME: *Signora* Trude, stay calm.

ANTONIO (*sarcastically*): We are civilized people.

PULICINO: And civilized or not, *we are working!*

TRUDE (*after a moment*): Nice work.

"Will you please, Ma'am, be quiet!" now sounded the sibilant voice of one of the Extras. My ancient dread of the wretched and impotent side of Humanity—or of what we take as such—now reasserted itself. Trude knew my feelings and smiled at my cowardice; she had a secret liking for the Extras, and it was nearly as though she had said to me: "I have nothing to fear from them, but perhaps *you* do!"

I was gripped by an indescribable cold, more real than the cold that entered through the window, where in any case the gaping hole had been covered by a great sheet of paper, which meshed with the sound outside of a whistle—a sibilance that might have been mistaken for a factory siren announcing a change of shift. But since there are no factories here, only woods, and since it wasn't an hour for work, but only for solitary blackbirds, just before dawn, that whistle could only mean, more or less, that the wail of the electric alarm had finally sprung to life.

I felt reanimated—or heartened—and once again I shut my eyes.

When I blinked them back open, I was certain that another TWENTY MINUTES had passed, but the siren had lapsed into silence by the end of the first sixty seconds.

The two *workers* were still at work, joined indeed by other strange figures who were coming and going and carrying away—I could not believe it!—the very window frames—since there was nothing else to take—and then the *shutters* and *blinds* and various scraps of cloth.

The sky above the woods was white.

At this point, suddenly, I reopened my eyes (which before I had simply imagined to be open) and now—finally awake is what I mean to say—I saw, as might be expected, that the Chamber of Night was empty. I knew, or believed I knew, that I had been dreaming. It was day, perhaps six in the morning; the chimney emitted a nameless plaint (since the wind had risen again) and everything was just as I had left it when I had fallen asleep in the *Grand-Mère*. The plastic curtain behind me was closed, the snob-class window was likewise closed, the radiator stone-cold. The *mausin* had retreated, but a dry north wind now shook the summits of the trees, bending them to and fro.

This, back then, was a period—I don't know if I have already mentioned it—when despite the good many hours I spent in my studio, I really had nothing to do. I was waiting for a letter, actually, a reply on which my peace of mind depended. What it said would allow me to decide whether or not I wanted to continue to live in this house in the woods. So my thoughts, while waiting for this letter, meandered through all the most various, and perhaps the saddest things—things, for example, like people stripping away from you, piece by piece, the house in which you live, and carting it all away.

I have dreamed, I said to myself, and yet some curious sensation of having been in touch with something real continued to stir inside of me—a feeling summoned by some of the figures seen in that dream. Not the girls, but Antonio and Pulicino. They seemed so ordinary and true-to-life as to make me wonder if by chance I hadn't seen their faces behind some shop counter or in some concierge's cage.

"Antonio and Pulicino! But I have met them! I have already seen them somewhere," I repeated to myself.

All morning long.

I went to the kitchen and met no special problems. The water had done no more damage than usual, and the floor had already dried. Abandonment and desolation, yes, but nothing, in short, that was new.

"And yet, I have met them!" I repeated to myself.

At eleven o'clock, no earlier, Signor Raggi finally arrived. He was quite a likable person, very outgoing and polite, and his ebullient chatter, typical of workers in the Capital, managed to distract me for an hour or two from my plaintive and doleful thoughts. He repaired the sink and conversed with Trude, who had come into the kitchen to keep an eye on things—she is always quite happy for a chance to talk with ordinary people, though as usual she hadn't so much as a spare glance for me—and finally, when it was already one o'clock in the afternoon, he left.

I went off to run a few errands for Trude down in the Arab Quarter at the bottom of the hill, and while returning up the road I felt very cold, and moreover so lost, Reader, in a mood of dark and inexplicable desperation, that I might— if I were a person of any courage, and if more than anything else I weren't so curious about the future—I might have decided to set myself on fire.

The wind had started again, and was quite intolerable. Trude had gone back to bed, and the whole house was empty and dark.

I no longer heard any *Toc* and *Tic* and *Ic* from the kitchen, but from everywhere a single:

OH! OH! OH!

During the past few days—spurred on, perhaps, by the open frame of mind that I've mentioned as surrounding my wait for the Letter—I had been highly absorbed in a series of philosophical readings, of which, as a secret to keep between us, it might just as well be said that I understood nothing at all. Yet even despite my lack of understanding—or perhaps precisely because of it—I was supremely engrossed by the things I was reading and they milled constantly in my mind. The person to whom you are listening is a woman of little education, and you are not to be misled by her occupation—shared today by many, if not indeed a multitude—as a mistress of the written word: the meanings of words, essentially, have always been a problem for me. I know how to write, but the true and proper summits of written thought (Aristotle, for example, or the great German philosophers) enchant me purely by way of their *sounds*. They remain, for me, so many walls of the courtyard of the Mind: and beyond them, over there, is the Rinascenza, the renascence of knowledge, while over here is the narrow compass of absence, which alone is the space I call my own.

This does nothing, however, to inhibit my soul's eternal certainty or intuition—just as anguish is eternal in my courtyard—of the world of the real: of Mathematics and Physics and, farther along, of the Principles and Laws (which would then—as I see it, or saw it—be the source of the trees and gentle breezes of our human Rinascenza). My utterly modest or indeed non-existent ego constantly circles such suspicions or uncertain certainties like a prisoner pacing back and forth; I feel that if only I comprehended some few parts of those Principles and Laws, my mind would grow calm, and then I could declare myself content within my courtyard.

So this was a period—owing perhaps to the unstable weather and the always more vehement Atlantic storms, or to certain sinister laments (the warnings from my devastated Kitchen) and various similar facts—when I found myself ever more frequently returning to obscure and difficult books. *What*, in short, I would ask myself, is the essence of the world; and *how*, on the one hand, does one have to look at things—the villas, the gardens, the woods—and,

132

on the other hand, at Trude, or at poverty, misery and quarantined courtyards; *who* presides over all of it; and *where* in it can one find a *purpose*, and *what* would that purpose be? There were thousands of such "silent" questions.

And since, as you'll surely remember, that dream of breaking and entering in the middle of the night was still quite fresh, and—furthermore—since neither Antonio nor Pulicino, almost as though they in fact were real people, had left my mind, I gave myself over (once again seated in the *Grand-Mère*) to the following thoughts:

"Admitting the existence of Antonio and Pulicino, and presuming them not to be plumbers, but True Thieves (as I suspect must somewhere exist), the very fact that the predicate of 'Thieves' can apply to them (to A. and P.) while allowing them still to remain *Antonio* and *Pulicino* is itself clear demonstration that the predicate with which they distinguish themselves belongs to the sphere of the mental Categories: and just as there is *honesty* and *rusticity*"— here I was thinking of Trude and of just how enormous she is—"there is certainly as well *their opposite*, which we can posit as Sub-honesty and Refinement," (inferior, according to my train of thought, to their root conditions—which here, precisely, were *honesty* and *rusticity*—since such roots were the matrices of being, whereas *Non-Honesty* and *Refinement* were nothing more that derivates).

But I don't intend to go any further with these truly impossible argumentations, a bit ridiculous as well, on Essences, Principles and Categories. I only want to show how melancholic my mind had grown, and how similar more or less to a labyrinth, on that First of March, at three o' clock—already!—in the afternoon.

Do they exist—Antonio and Pulicino—or did I only dream them? And what would be the Category—if in fact they exist—to which to ascribe their power over the soul? And are there only two such creatures, or two thousand, or billions? Don't they stand perhaps at the Origin—or are they not the Origin itself—of *everything?* And with that particular thought, recognizably sick and delirious, I felt myself grow faint, and ready to die.

Meanwhile a true and proper whirlwind was battering down on the Woods, as though to expunge it. The Wood and the Tempest embraced, forming a single cloud of gold and fog from which flew out dried leaves (from the previous fall) like arrows of blood. This clamor of swords and ferocious laments prevented me from hearing the squeak of the gate which I might quite easily—through the snob-class window—have observed; but still I caught sight of, yes, *two* mailmen who advanced from precisely that direction, heads hung low.

Just as they reached a position that directly faced my vantage point—my seat in the *Grand-Mère*—they raised up onto the tips of their run-down shoes, or so I imagine them. Their caps at least had presented a note of something shabby and worn; and from the hint of pallor and poverty transpiring from beneath the beaks of those caps, I recognized my two nocturnal acquaintances, Antonio and Pulicino.

Above the wall at the balcony's edge, a hand was by now reaching upwards and hovered in the air behind the window pane: a hand—five brown fingers, quite plainly—which then dropped a letter.

Next, just as they had come, the two "mailmen" departed.

Amazement and joy so thoroughly overcame me—yes, my mind's unconscious felt even a turbid joy in this real and actual encounter with something it had held to be a dream or a shadow—that for a moment I thought no more about the letter.

Indeed, for quite a few moments.

But then, on recovering, I flew to open the balcony door, picked up the letter, and rushed just as quickly back to my seat in the *Grand-Mère*. I had been chilled by the cold north wind, but my heart now pounded for wholly different reasons.

Again I had seen the two Thieves, Antonio and Pulicino! And they had been *costumed* as mailmen.

The letter, as you're sure to understand, attentive Reader, was no longer of the slightest importance to me. My mind was engaged by only one fact: that during the night I had not dreamed; that I had neither had visions nor walked in my sleep; that Antonio and Pulicino—the Thieves— *existed*, which also proved the existence of the Categories, of Order, of the sacred Principle of Category. And before too long I'd probably comprehend an even more basic reality that precedes all philosophy: the fact that the essence of the world is theft.

"Who is that letter from? Who has written you a letter? I've just heard the mailman." Madame Trude's voice, from behind the curtain, feigned fatigue.

"Nobody," I said. And then, intending to frighten her, "It's the telephone bill."

And in fact there was fear in her voice as she asked, "How big is it?"

"Well…I haven't looked yet…but it can't be much…." And then, after a moment, without having opened the letter, "Forty."

Trude in person then peered through the curtain:

"And who's to pay it? Me? Give it here!" Her demand was quite energetic.

I picked up an old phone bill from the mantle above the fireplace (my conscience reproved me, but she was too excited for me to be able to talk with her, or to find another way out) and then handed it to her through the curtain as she propped her glasses on her nose. I could hear her unfold the scrap of paper, and then she said, obscurely pacified:

"It's a bit less than forty."

But at that point, I was no longer listening.

"On the date...So and so, Inc...etcetera etcetera.... Sir! Your Excellence!"—that was the greeting, without a name—"We take the pleasure, by this present letter, of taking the opportunity of duly informing you that this Building's Owners and Administration, in consideration and repeated examination of the Circumstances at the time of said Building's construction, and thus of the geological *restlessness* of the terrain on which it stands...(etcetera etcetera), and having further determined the hazard of such terrain, and as well the *unfortunate* contingencies that the Building itself may at any moment suffer as a consequence, and therefore as well of the inconvenience that would therefrom derive for the Holders of Absolute Title themselves— in respect of the norms established by Law in relation to Leaser security, and as clearly approved (etcetera etcetera) by the competent Legal Forum, said holders of title have determined...etcetera etcetera, with a deliberation of the date of...and...duly communicated to Your Excellence, to proceed to the abrogation of any and all contracts—no matter how regularly stipulated—signed between itself and your Excellence, and thereafter to the Building's demolition. Your Excellence is thereby requested etcetera etcetera to be so kind, at the lapse of the minimum period prescribed by Law (!), to vacate all rooms on the premises of the House in the Woods, which minimum period is established in the no longer extendable extent of THREE days!

"With all best wishes and the sincerest expression of our gratitude, etcetera etcetera."

Considerable gloom overshadowed the part of my mind that could still make objective assessments, and it assessed that I was sleeping! That I had fallen back into the be-witched slumber of the house. And the reason for such a conclusion, Reader, was very simple: not only was this letter *overflowing* with grammatical errors (my transcription has somewhat cleaned it up) and written in a style that no serious landlord (such as the owners of the House in the Woods) would have ever used, but as well its pages bore traces of *brown* fingers. So these phantoms, Antonio and Pulicino, had not *delivered* the letter. They had *authored* it. And since Antonio and Pulicino (here I'm at the heart of the matter) were dream people, as proven by the fact that the light of morning in the Chamber of Night had shown no remaining trace of them, I could only conclude I had also seen these mailmen in a dream; which, in turn, was proof— since the letter was still in my hands—that *I had not yet awakened.*

So when, then, would I finally reopen my eyes?

I also pondered another question. I wondered if I hadn't perchance been sleeping for the *whole* of my life— ever since I had first begun to admire the created world (Nature, more than anything else, which was why I had come to live in this House in the Woods, and much to Trude's ire, since she loved the company of neighbors), and I asked myself what would become of us, of me and Trude (whose real name I have not spoken) if I were *not* to wake up.

"Ah," I complained, while trying to light the fire, "why should my lot have been sleep. Why have I seen and fixed the basis of everything in sleep and dream, while life all around me has lived and lives in fervor, with Life and Works, Ideas and Motors, all in Alacrity and Plain Reality?

"Why am I afflicted with this sinister vision of a Thief who governs the world, while life itself flowers and the seasons revolve *without compunction?* The world is full of generosity; nature flows on as a gift to rats and angels; contemplative serenity is denied to me alone. I alone, in fact, saw Antonio and Pulicino; and now I read their vulgar lies." So with a gesture of rebellion, I threw the letter into the fire.

I watched it burn, and I was once again awake!

Night arrived and a drizzle no less vexed and vexing than my state of mind (or at least its visible part) came along with it and knocked at the windowpanes.

Now all green and decked with pearls (raindrops) the Woods were pleasant to look at and helped me in some undefinable way. I felt that the wind, now much more bland and blowing from the southwest, had gone as soft and gentle as I had known it to be in my childhood, and I was thrown by that thought into a state of mind so tremulous and tender that I'll make no attempt to relate it. So even in spite of a slight cold (but tears as well ran down beside my nose), and despite as well having gone out already in the morning, I wanted to go out again. And immediately did. Having called good-bye to Trude through the folding screen and warned her to open the door *to no one*, I took up umbrella and rain coat and went *weeping* towards the door of the vestibule. I mention these tears since usually I never cry at all; crying is utterly foreign to me; so these tears both alarmed and secretly moved me.

Shortly—imagine my relief!—I found myself beyond the gate, out in the lane I described at the start. It was evening—or night (every now and then these phases of the day would alternate, often it seemed still early in the afternoon, or dawn)—so the path through the woods was deserted. I halted, as though in a French novel of the end of the eighteenth century, next to a minuscule grave hidden in the shadow of a bush; and I remembered that this was the grave of a certain *Lucino*, a cat I once long ago had adopted and nursed. All to no avail! Lucino had been black and white, and his head, the first time I saw him, from behind, seemed connected to his body *by a thread*—his neck was just that thin—and it was covered by shiny black *hair*, as though by a wig; but when he turned—he was tied to a branch—his *peaceful* eyes aroused my pity; they were just that distant. He seemed to speak to me, but in a subtle, strange, unknown and indecipherable language in which every now and then he would timidly ask why he had been born a cat and why he had suffered and now had to die. All very silently.

So here I am, dreaming again, I said to myself, or, to put it better, raking about in the past and among First Causes! Ah, Lucino, please be still!

After walking the length of the avenue, I suddenly noticed that a small lopsided creature, small and quiet, was ahead of me, I mean preceding me, and I was certain it had to be Lucino. Night had fallen as I walked along the road, but on skirting the corner of the house—which juts forward, as I said at the start, like a cascade of rock towards the Rinascenza—I could see that the creature, always bobbing and moving on a slant like the shade of a cat, had slipped into the courtyard before the garage, the door of which, painted green, seemed from that point of view to be closed. And there the figure had disappeared.

Curiosity—with as well a sense of excitement, but

curiosity was strong—prodded me on; I wanted to follow the creature.

I too entered the courtyard, and then pushed against the door of the garage.

Here, quite clearly, I was no longer dreaming, because a good twenty automobiles—nicely polished and indeed resplendent with their various colors of lacquer and the whiteness of their headlights—stood out in the vastness of the shadowy garage, at the back of which was a squarish patch of green-orange light. Surely that had to be the sunset sky, flushing through the famous little window in my courtyard. What, however, is one to think about a sunset here in the courtyard when it was night on the path in the woods? Well, that's hardly a cause for amazement, since Time—as the Reader well knows—and even Space—is only the reflection of a state of mind.

I decided to advance and take a look as to whether the flood from the pipes in my kitchen had caused any damage here.

Having reached what should have been the spot, I saw that the floor, of beaten earth, was totally dry.

My eyes then turned towards the sewage pipe that drained the building. Rising up rather like a tower that lost itself in the ceiling, it showed a small open hatch just about three feet from the ground—a small open hatch outpouring a blinding rush of light.

I remained, Reader, quite breathless.

This light, Reader, resembled the light of a thousand diamonds displayed on a pink satin cushion; but an instant later the cushion was purple, then a vivid green, and then reverted to its first dazzling white. And the rain of diamonds, since a rain is truly what it was, continued!

Quite clearly it flowed into the sewage pipe from a second pipe, or a gutter—its upper part buried deep inside the wall and therefore hidden—that emitted a constant low-voiced *whish* mixed with the sound of a silvery tinkling, like crystalline rain on a silver tray; and as the shower rushed down past the hatch in the tower, it left it encrusted with those pure, fleeting, and multicolored lights that had blinded me, and that blinded me still.

Every now and then, a stone of a paradisiacal light flew out and landed on the garage's filthy floor, there to dissolve into a tiny puddle, strangely dark and displaying no further luster.

And there were times when a dark thin hand, quite plainly gloved in black leather, would catch some one of these marvelous stones as they flew through the air, then tossing them back into the hatch, where they resumed their downward plunge.

Automatically—finally—I lifted my eyes, which for a while had been riveted, with the bewitched curiosity that grips us in dreams, on the small hatch door; and there beside it was a typically human shadow, if that phrase makes any sense, leaning elegantly on an elbow against the tower, while his other hand—he was the Stoker of the Dream—gripped a storied silver shovel.

The orange light from the window in the courtyard—the always bricked-up window that now was no longer bricked up—was the principal source of the "joy" which illumined that face: and a face, you're please to pardon my exaggeration, of a beauty not to be found in any scheme or model of recent human culture ("anthropomorphic," rather than "human," would be a less graceful word) and perhaps just barely perceptible in ancient Persian miniatures. The dawn light and the agony that hung around the contours of the lower part of the face were doubtless due to the flickering astral fulgor of the furnace.

Myskin, or M'Yskin—that is the time-honored name, and it might just as well be spoken right away, no matter that the person who bore it may seem (or may not) to be a vision or a vague reminiscence—was dressed, moreover, in a fairly curious way. He wore a black mesh tunic that disappeared at the ankles into a pair of striped boots, and another odd article of clothing consisted of a head covering—call it a black cap with a visor—the summit of which was adorned by a roundish light. So it was owing to the cap, tipped down over his eyes, that one found it so hard to discern the rest of his face. All one clearly saw were the chin and the mouth, held in a melancholy smile, and behind that mouth the frequent glimpse, inexplicably, of a sudden shadow. Two long ear-rings, each in the shape of a half moon and set with three turquoise stones, dangled from his left ear; affixed to his right ear by a green stem (but *naturally*, meaning that it grew from the ear itself) was a bunch of two or three pink geraniums.

On his arm (and I must not forget a thin golden cord that two or three times encircled his waist) he carried a cape, or shawl, of which there is nothing I can say. It was a waterfall of moonlight in a green May night. Whether made of some real or dreamed material, or of heavenly or underground fires, is something I will never know.

On his chest, Reader, as though seen through a tiny pane of mica, one noted a heart, much smaller than normal, but utterly real, even though made of beaten silver; that was clear from its rhythmic beating: its rhythm was calm and serene.

This creature, who showed not a single flaw either in the cut of his figure or in the highly proper bearing that bespoke his belonging to an *extremely* elevated class, did not, moreover, seem at all tired by his work—neither tired nor repelled nor in any way intrigued And I could see meanwhile that at his feet there crawled the ghost—or so I have to imagine—of the departed Lucino. And the regal figure seemed not so much to put up with this feline ghost, than rather to consider it familiar.

As I shaped this thought, I also heard myself addressed by a voice, no less cordial than shaded with irony.

"Were you looking for Lucino?"

I would have wanted to reply, but couldn't. I also found myself thinking, "Why should he be so ironic, and what does this cordiality mean? Where does this creature come from? Who is this Myskin, *really?*"—not at all surprised that I knew his name—when in the wink of an eye everything vanished. The courtyard window was again bricked up, the sewage pipe was dark and cold, and the gentleman in black, along with Lucino, was no longer there.

My mind was quite heavy as I left the garage and found my way back to the path in the woods.

Shortly later, in the Kitchen in Decrepitude—which however, luckily enough, was no longer losing water—I made myself two eggs, sunny-side up. Trude, on the other hand, insisted that I make French toast for her, which I did, and then I took it to her room. (She was wide awake and had found out my trick with the phone bill, so she wasn't speaking with me.) Then I returned to the kitchen, which was the only place where Trude and her bothering never followed me and where I could taste the unspeakable joy (when I wasn't at work) of being a bit alone. Carrying a blanket and the *Prolegomena*, I went to install myself on a very tall stool right next to the Major Chest of drawers. While reading, and as night was falling, I had a view of a part of the courtyard and the woods that towered up beyond its wall. Here—I had also brought along my watch—*two or three hours* went by without any sign that the night, by now far advanced, might suffocate the evening's always more cheerless twilight. And the silence, Reader, was enormous! The Woods—I could hear it all the way over here, at the back of the house—were *murmuring*; and those other stands of trees on the grounds of the Rinascenza were ceaselessly shaking their heads (the heads they seemed to have in that livid light) and even their arms...and Clouds passed by, again and again, at times dragging with them a few gold stars, timid and amazed...creatures perhaps but a few years old.

It wasn't raining, but it threatened to rain. And high up above, there was conflict, I could feel it, a conflict resulting yet again from the oceanic storms which had newly discovered a channel to the East (since the masses of colder air had withdrawn). But they encountered an impediment: thanks precisely to a kind of collapse on the part of the masses of polar air, a powerful wind now whistled in from the East, laden with melancholy stories. So, in short, there were now two winds, the East Wind and the West Wind—while the South Wind (not the *mausin*, which *slept*) remained in abeyance—that contended for the region of the sky above the area where I live. And all, I repeat, in silence! Because I couldn't consider the low-toned whistling and the sad and broken muttering of the two Winds to be human voices (even if that is what they seemed to be). Finally, however, the South Wind, which until then had only *murmured*, sprang back to life and prevailed along with the East Wind. The darkness of the storm receded, withdrawing northwards! The moon appeared, and smiled at me. A cloud, gilded by the light of that moon, passed quickly above the Courtyard, as though searching for someone she knew. I heard a tiny patter of rapid, dancing steps: fresh rain! My heart seemed to open, and I cried this time in earnest.

But you mustn't imagine, Reader, that the feelings I felt were good. I cried with terror, with rage, with a melancholy that voiced my reaction to the injustice I seemed to see in the world, or that resulted from it. I had seen the diamonds! And whether or not I had seen them in a dream made no difference. I had seen them all the same. They were all the freedom and happiness and beauty of the world that lay behind the courtyard, and debarred to me.

Aloft on my stool in the solitary kitchen, I now cried in torrents, and finally I picked up my Kant again and began—out of rage, not at all knowing what in fact I was doing—to eat one of its pages. There was nothing I could any longer make of Principles and Ideas. I wanted a few of those diamonds for myself. I picked up a scrap of paper and a yellow pencil that served in Trude's pathetic kitchen for jotting down the shopping lists, and as though possessed (giving up on devouring Kant) I started doing sums... ridiculous, delirious sums. I calculated, in short, that if Myskin had given me only A SINGLE DIAMOND, from that flow of diamonds that had rained down the drain pipe, that if I clutched it in my hands and ran into the city, to the best jeweller, and sold it, I would have come away, in cash, (these were the thoughts of my weakened mind) with at least some *fifty* million *reis!* (My deranged and unsteady mind was convinced that I was somewhere in a Portuguese territory—perhaps passing through.) It was quite enough—the figures were just that clear—to be instantly exchanged for a modest villa, like *Landon House*, with a garden and curtains at the windows, and all in the midst of endless flowering meadows. Lucino was still alive (I couldn't yet be sure, but I dared nonetheless to shape the thought) and I would ask him to come and live with me. Trude would have a pretty room on the garden, large, with all of her bric-a-brac, and an entrance of her own (by way of the terrace) to go to the village and remain in touch with the People. We'd have been so very happy.

These thoughts, and the feeling *it could all come true*, and setting myself to adding up sums on that piece of paper were all one thing; but when I had finished all my arithmetic, wholly astray in meanders of peace and happiness, I saw—from the color of the sky—that this again was a melancholy evening of I didn't know what year. The diamond was forgotten, along with Myskin, the house, all those *reis*, and happiness as well.

"Oh, whatever is this world all about?" The question returned again and again, in a torrent of invincible weakness through a failing heart where worlds and dreams, past and future (not my own, Reader) were forever in alternation, like the nervous winds in the March night sky. I abandoned the stool, and went over toward the balcony.

It was daytime, or seemed to be; all two thousand of the Courtyard's grey and white bricks were wrapped like a household apron around the wall, now seeming to be made of pearl, which divided the Courtyard from the Rinascenza. And a light was aloft in the sky, not the moon, though of pure gold...a bizarre light that moved slowly among the last clouds. It was a kite! Trailing down behind it was a golden thread, or a small cord. Printed on the kite was a flag in brilliant colors, designating the country of _____, and the thread dropped down to within only a few feet of my courtyard.

I opened the balcony door, impulsively, and began to descend the steps.

But I managed no more than a single step. What faced me was just that amazing!

Myskin—though now he wore no ornaments, except

for a light on his forehead—lay sleeping or resting at the foot of those steps.

His silver heart, behind the mica visor, had almost ceased to beat. Decked with flowers it might have been a miniscule river barge—flowers that skipped and danced, flowing like waves. Yet the silver heart itself had almost ceased to beat.

One of his legs lay outstretched, the other bent backwards; his arms were raised to his head, and framed it, but his face was hidden. He slept!

There are moments in the life of the imagination—which, after all, is the life that all of us live—when everything you have ever thought before, even an instant before, is no longer of any importance, or at least stands perfectly still, and the only thing you see is reality. Yet the real, in that very instant, shows an unexpected dimension of itself...becoming everything one never might have thought Reality to be...while consisting all the same of all the most humble marks of the here and now.... But I do not want, and perhaps might not be able, to say anything more.

Myskin, now, for me, was only a young man who had fainted, for reasons that didn't intrigue me, while happening to find himself in my courtyard. I studied his slender build (entirely of *this* world, so perhaps he was a dancer) and the vacant face, as though of marble, which lay turned in the direction of the kite. His princely hands were open, and the flowers continued to flow across his breast.... But I allowed myself no illusions: his heart, now, had ceased to beat.

In my bewilderment, "Trude!" was the only word that came to mind.

It was drizzling. I took the blanket from around my shoulders and bent down to spread it over the corpse. But something held me back, some inexplicable childhood anguish.

Trude, having been summoned, not certainly by my voice, but rather, I'd say, by her instinct, had come to the window of *my* room.

"Leave it alone," she said, "it must have fallen from upstairs."

Trude's voice, for anyone who truly knew her, held not so much as a trace of deception. Trude was Reality itself. Myskin, to Trude's eyes—Myskin the stoker of the dream, the prince of constellations of diamonds and the brother beyond all doubt of sweet-voiced Israfel—was nothing more than a bed-side mat that had fallen from an upstairs floor!

"Later I'll take it to the janitor," she added.

And closed the window.

My tears were finished, but had left me with a feeling of suffocation. I would never, ever, know Myskin's generosity. A single diamond, only a single diamond, and my life would have been transformed! He was dead! And that wasn't all. An emotion from very far away, and very humble, was aroused by my sight of this lifeless man, and this is why I had not dared to spread my old blanket on top of him. He seemed to belong to the world of the winds and storms and inscrutable elements—as light as the trade winds, as pure as your childhood dreams while watching the dawn. And now he no longer existed. The diamonds, yes; but the Rule himself, the supreme source—now I understood—of the beauties and peace of the Rinascenza, the key to all mystery—what had been known as Myskin, the stoker of splendor—I was never to see him again.

I remembered how he had said "Were you looking for Lucino?" and again I burst into plentiful tears. The memory of the diamonds and the certainty of their loss were now almost without importance.

At that point, Lucino, in spirit—but I could also say *in person*—came to rub up against me. He looked now at me, now at Myskin, now at the sky.

"But what's wrong, my dear?" I said, following his gaze.

I watched Lucino's eyes—veiled and seemingly blue— as they turned toward the sky. Looking in that direction, I saw the kite I mentioned before. With its flag of the nation, and trailing a cord, it now descended.

Suspended from that gilt cord were two thin men, fully dressed. Perhaps they were acrobats, and they were smiling.

The tiny vessel continued to descend, ever further downward.

My soul's sad phantasies had once again stumbled to a halt. Something was missing. And there, as the doctors of pain would say, lay the root of the evil, the void that causes pain; and this void was a lack of knowledge. What was missing was the Kant I had chewed up and swallowed.

Not the *Prolegomena*; no, not that at all! And finally— I too was seated on the steps—it seemed, Reader, quite clear to me (while keeping the company of the dead prince and intentionally ignoring the kite, and absentmindedly scratching Lucino's back) that a synthesis of Kant was really quite simple, of Kant and of all the various philosophies that stood before or to the back of *him* and that opened us up to this world. It was actually right before me, simply to reach out and touch, if only I could manage to remember what's called *infantilidad*. What, good man, do you want from *infantilidad?* And you, good woman? Perhaps those Diamonds? No, you want no more than the reappearance of the winds, of the stars, of the kites in the stillness of the mornings of the autumn and the spring. And this song of a blackbird, so entirely moving, from behind the Woods. Listen! Listen! And shed no tears, even if Trude has told you that nothing but a throw-rug has fallen from a balcony rail and she'll give it to the janitor as soon as the hour is decent. This, good woman, is the world: a thing made of wind and gentle voices—made of waiting for apparitions and nostalgia for the loss of them, made of things *that are not the world.*

My meditations had resumed!

Trude appeared at the kitchen door.

"Coffee," she announced.

I went back into the house, but not entirely. One eye remained on the courtyard, the other on the kite, which by now was directly in front of the kitchen window.

"It's about to rain again," said Trude, seeing that the air was hazy.

She left the kitchen—my eyes followed her movements as she went—and as soon as she was gone I saw Myskin at the modest balcony window. He was alive and his forehead was fully visible, but I allowed myself no illusions. It as only his well-mannered ghost.

I cannot describe what lay within his face, calm and vivacious all at once, both of death to Reality, and of greater Reality. He wasn't crying, *but he had* cried. He gazed in my direction and made a sign with two fingers that I should open the window a bit…. He had something to tell me….

I felt myself go pale.

Directly behind him, the two men from the vessel were collecting a slender body dressed in black. An arm and the lovely face hung down across the shoulder of one of the bearers as they loaded it onto the vessel. They departed. But a second Myskin was still at the kitchen door, *nodding and making a sign*. He held his palms extended, bearing in each of them a diamond. One hand, his right hand, continually dropped its diamond into the other and another always reappeared in its place; the one in his left hand dissolved into a drop of black water!

I recalled the figures of the Rebuses; throttled by emotion, I could not speak.

Myskin then slowly withdrew, stepping backward towards the Courtyard, sometimes looking at me—with a brother's compassion—sometimes at the sky.

I believe that the Kite, or unreal vessel, took no more than a second to depart. But for a quarter of an hour I continued to see it, immobile and golden, against the tattered background of a rain cloud. The second Myskin continued all along to take his leave of me with that act of compassion—as distant and gentle as the peace that's known to children—while the first lay stretched upon the ground.

And what did all of this mean?

At eight in the morning—it was no longer raining and a clear March sky had in fact quite plainly asserted itself— one of the people who lived upstairs (Mrs. Verdi on the third floor) actually came to pick up a throw-rug or a bedside mat of fairly noteworthy age. Mrs. Verdi also took the chance to stop—for the very first time in her life—for a chat with Trude.

"Well, yes...there was a bit of damage, in the garage...the sewer pipe, quite literally smashed."

"Thieves?" asked the ingenuous Trude.

"*Signora!*" cried Mrs. Verdi. "Surely I hope you can't

imagine that vast amounts of capital are running through the sewage pipes!"

"But people, yes!" came *Signora* Trude's reply, obstinate and no less surreal.

"*People?* What do you mean by that?"

"Madam! I'll say no more!"

I was all ears.

"No," said Mrs. Verdi. "*Now*, you really must go on. You've already gone a bit too far!"

"Madam, *capital is people*."

"I beg your pardon?"

"Yes, since it's Facts, Abuses, and Work (and not-Work), *capital is people*. And with that, I don't owe you one more word."

"I think you're trying to offend me!"

"Well, there's nothing much I can do about that!" said Trude. And energically shut the door.

This foolish conversation—of a clearly political stamp —was of no interest to me. My heart still dwelt on the dead prince, and on his task as stoker of the fires—and on his kindness, both while alive and dead. But all these double and treble visions had left me far too out of sorts to feel anything other than wildly appreciative of Trude's disconnected phrases.

A moment later I joined her on the terrace.

"Granny," I said, dear *Grand-Mère*, please. Just a word, and I'll never again interrupt you when you want to be alone."

"Hurry up with it."

"What does that mean: *capital is people*?"

Trude approached me, with that eternally benevolent and allusive air she had in the moments when her sensibility, something she in fact possessed, was most acute. She raised her arm and landed a slap like a wooden stave on my right cheek.

"That'll teach you to ask stupid questions!"

"Oh, excuse me, *Signora* Trude!"

And I woke up once again.

At this point—my story is almost finished and the Reader can feel reassured, since I didn't again fall asleep or dream any more—the only thing left for me to do was to think and think some more, attempting to discover an explanation for all of these charades. But let's be reasonable! How was all this possible? My head was utterly empty and befuddled: the sewer, Lucino, and the Regulatory Prince were a pain that refused to go away.

A perfectly calm and azure day arrived, and from behind the snob-class window I watched the same few fellow tenants. Workmen passed by on their way to repair the sewer—preceded by the janitor. A *real mailman* went upstairs, to the fourth floor, with a special delivery letter and a bouquet of flowers for the Marquis. The girl from the second floor went out, on her bike, with friends.

The woods were brightly golden.

A few vacationing birds were in song.

A day, and a series of days, like every other was clearly at hand.

I remembered that a corner of my library, at the end of the Hallway of Fears, held a book of Persian fables; and with the very greatest horror (reality having resurfaced) I recalled it to contain a bizarre account of a certain Mysrafel (or M'Ysrafel), a benevolent Genius of the Night. I went to fetch the book, turned on a table lamp, and feverishly searched for the little tale. In fact, it was only a few lines long and contained the whole of the story I have narrated:

God entrusted a certain Mysrafel (or M'Ysrain?), a creature of celestial beauty and goodness, with the harvest of the human souls who are *unable*, for some reason or another, to reach the heavens, or who are destined to feed the earth. These are the souls of the Powerful, even if in life they were good. Such souls are collected at the moment of death (according to my Persian tale) in portentous tubings, and sent along an always underground course to their destination: which was the manure pile (and to serve as manure) at the Wondrous Gardens, where they are then to take the form of trees, flowers, and fruits. At first, at the moment of death, they were nothing but *Diamonds*—as they had always been in life—hard Stones of pulchritude, power, and wealth. But afterwards, at death, rushing through those tubes, they finally turned into liquids and then flowed out to nourish the gardens of the earth, in which, after all, they had believed.

The Persians had such odd imaginations!

I don't know if it was right of me, but at a certain point I was no longer interested. I took quite melancholy note of two things: first, that everything I had seen—or believed to see—which is practically the same—*was not my own*. In second place: that these Persian stories are lacking in logic, just as they lack conclusions.

Why ever, in fact, had poor M'Ysrain been chosen for such a task? And why, for such a task, do we have to be told of his "goodness"?

Perhaps, I remarked to myself, those gardens are places of punishment, ultra-earthly places; and the whole of this inexplicable world is a mixture of earth and ultra-earth; and all conditions, in this world, exist side by side. And what you believe to be *privilege* has no future; while things that have *no* future are perhaps real privilege!

I remembered Lucino's desperation when I had found him long ago, half strangled and tied to a tree. I had attempted to save him, and while dying he had looked at me so sweetly. And Lucino—though only in dream!—was still alive, and dear to the Prince, who indeed had carried him away with him; whereas these endless gardens that surrounded the House in the Woods were mute and full of pain, and how very inexplicable and anguishing!

Cemeteries of Diamonds.

But—another question—why had Myskin (who seemed to be immortal) died? The answer, here, wasn't very hard to find: he had harvested too much, far too much pain. He was the brother *par excellence*, tender and compassionate as desired by God—just as clouds are damp and the moon bright with massive gold. Out of tenderness and far too ancient sorrow, he had not been able to bear it.

Perhaps—please don't think me presumptuous, Reader—perhaps I too, by way of my night of anger and desperation, had given him pain.

I see myself again before the sewage pipe—even though only in dream—with my eyes agape and arid, my hand held ready.... He had gently smiled....

But why (come to think of it) was the tubing of the sewer now *actually* broken?

That, Reader—since I'm no longer recalling dreams, but actual facts—is a subject that allows for no doubts. I heard the story from Vincent, our janitor (and a man who knows about money) as he later pointed his amply-ringed hand at the spot where the damage had been repaired.

His smile, his calm, and the sight of his rings made me shudder....

But enough, we've had enough of hallucinations.

It strikes me, however, as indispensable, before concluding, to say a few words about the two scoundrels named Antonio and Pulicino, who were the janitors of a neighboring building. So, there was every good reason for my seeming to have *recognized* them.

The police arrested Antonio and Pulicino Fanella, from the city of _____ in the Province of Avellino, for various other thefts, and their jumbled confessions (their intelligence was well beneath the norm) happened to touch on the story of the forged letter they had sent to me, announcing my eviction. In my confusion I had taken it for a vision. They had hoped, afterward, to be able to rent my ground-floor courtyard apartment, since the closet beneath the stairs, according to them, contained a *secret passage* into the garage (a kind of walled-up closet that led down to the sewer pipe, where I had seen the angel—or the Prince of departed souls—Myshkin.)

They said that the sewage pipe (and this, to believe my dreams, might well be true) had a *hatch* in it, where every now and then one could see a precipitous rush of diamonds that came from all the parts of the Capital. They insisted that the two of them were far from greedy and would have been satisfied with only a handful.

"And where, gentlemen," at this point queried the Judge, as the papers reported, in a quite facetious tone, "where were all of these diamonds supposed to go?"

They didn't know what to say.

Careful investigation of the lower part of the sewage pipe was later to reveal, along with all the blasted filaments of filth that the sewage contained, an *iridescent* substance, well known to chemistry, but the name of which I don't remember. It comes from all the soaps that housewives throw into basins and sinks, and it amply explained the error that the two rascals had made.

I saw them again, a few months after their release from prison, and they deserve a few kind words, if only in the name of the dreams to which they appealed and in the midst of which they passed their lives. It was in May, on a day shot through with a silver drizzle, and the whole of the landscape as calm and enigmatic as a lily of the fields.

They didn't look very well. Antonio had been ill, and Pulicino's left eye had had too close a brush with a piece of hot iron and was nearly blind. He had covered it with a patch of cloth, a filthy patch of red cloth.

Here is our conversation:

"Well, how are things going?" I asked (not without sarcasm).

"We have to ask you to forgive us, *Signora*."

"Now you know very well that there's no such thing as a *Signora*," bitterly, "who has no money."

"And yet, *Signora*, you let a really fine chance get away from you!" Antonio, humbly.

"What chance?"

Pulicino, imagining to see me better, took off his red patch, and I saw that poor half-blind eye he had.

"That," he replied, fixing me with a tremendous stare, but nonetheless humbly and as though distressed, "is something it's better not to talk about."

"Are you referring *to the wind?*" I asked, after a moment's hesitation, knowing I was babbling, and while thinking back to the Kite. Both of them, to my great surprise, ingenuously nodded "yes." I could have flown away — they said — to somewhere far from this earth, and *I hadn't taken advantage of it.*

"That," after a moment of silence, "means that you were *watching*. And where were you?..."

"Down by the window, beneath the stairs, we were watching, *Signora*...."

"Well..." I said, "well..." feeling endlessly perturbed. After all, I felt ashamed of myself.

"That's how it was, Ma'am," said Antonio. "You taught us a lesson: you could have gone off to Heaven, but you didn't think of it."

I saw that these two humble figures—rags of humanity, discards of nothingness, one of them in awful health, and the other with his disfigured face—were a great deal more sensitive and more full of dreams than a lady of letters who eats her Kant. In everything that had happened, they had lived out their part with humble rapacity, and thus with faith.

"Were you planning, that night, to rob me?" I asked, confusing (once again!) dream and reality.

To my great surprise:

"Miss Trude was in on it."

"In on it?"

"She wanted to teach you a lesson—wake you up a bit—and she called us in...paid us.... But not that we'd have come away with nothing.... You know how it is, *Signora*."

I wasn't surprised about Trude—I knew her quite well. Reality is the way it is; I smarted only from having let myself be fooled.

"Well," I said, "well."

I wanted to ask something about the King of the Dead, the noble M'Ysrain-Myskin, the one who in the legend (and in reality) overlooks the passage of souls from Power to humble earthly nourishment, and thus to the world's sad flowering; but I felt that here I should say no more. Surely he had to be in Heaven; or in our own poor heads—Antonio's, Pulicino's, and mine—if it was true that all three of us had only dreamed.

We said good-bye to one another quite simply. Antonio and Pulicino remained seated on the doorstep, between two vases of brightly-colored geraniums—of such a sharp and excruciating color, Reader!—and I set off *alone* along the path through the woods.

As said before, it was a sleepy May morning. The sky was veiled with silver; all the trees and shrubs around me in the admirable region of the Rinascenza sparkled like eyes, like hearts that remember, and regret.

I stopped at the side of Lucino's grave. I thought about my poor strangled creature and his misery, and I reflected that the poor too are animals: animals hanged and strangled by their poverty, or caught in that river of life and wealth that drags them always further on, finally to death and an indistinguishable grave.... But perhaps, I thought, in those country graves, the graves of the world's poor souls...perhaps nothing is any longer there.... They have gone somewhere else, to a heavenly reward at the side of divine M'Ysrain. These earthly solitudes, so full of terror, are a place they will never visit again.

There was a small geranium—which I had never noticed before—beside Lucino's grave.

I stopped to touch it.

* * *

Before too long I decided to move. (I write these last few lines, as surely you intuit, in a different house.) The House in the Woods was a place that no longer appealed to me. But I have always remembered Lucino's grave, beneath the shrub, and sometimes in dreams I again see all those clouds, I re-hear the cry of the winds. I again see the moon above the courtyard, the moon that descended towards the house to collect *someone*. Again I see that someone lying close to the stairs, sick or dead like our childhood, and then beckoning a moment later from behind the window panes... pointing at the sky and the dawn with his fleshless, pure, and regal hand....